SHADOWS IN THE FOG

A MURDER. A TOWN. A DETECTIVE'S OBSESSION.

NIKUNJ

Made with ♥ on the Notion Press Platform
www.notionpress.com

Contents

Prologue   v

  1. The Body In The River   1

  2. The Detective And The Past   3

  3. A Town With Secrets   5

  4. Threads Of Deception   7

  5. The Missing Witness   9

  6. A Killer's Game   12

  7. The Confession That Wasn't   15

  8. Truth Beneath The Lies   19

  9. The Final Hunt   23

10. Justice In The Dark   27

11. A New Case Begins   31

12. A Killer's Calling Card   34

13. A Trail Of Ghosts   38

14. The Hunter And The Hunted   41

15. Blood In The Shadows   46

16. No Safe Haven   50

17. The Enemy Within   54

18. Closing The Noose   59

19. The Tipping Point   64

20. Into The Fire   68

21. The Fall Of The Architect   71

22. The Ghost That Wouldn't Die   74

23. A Game Of Shadows   76

Contents

24. Smoke And Ashes   79

25. A Trail Of Blood   82

26. The Betrayal   85

27. A Flight Into Darkness   88

28. Wreckage And Ruin   91

29. The Silent Hour   94

30. No Way Out   97

31. Ashes And Echoes   101

32. The Gathering Storm   105

33. The Last Move   108

34. Endgame Begins   112

35. The Final Gambit   115

36. The Last Stand   119

Epilogue – The Cost of Shadows   123

Prologue

A Cry in the Night

The wind howled through the dense trees, rustling the brittle autumn leaves that littered the ground. Moonlight shimmered on the river's surface, casting eerie shadows along the muddy banks. Somewhere in the distance, an owl hooted, breaking the oppressive silence that had settled over the town of Ridgewood.

Emily Carter ran.

Her breath came in short, desperate gasps, her sneakers slipping on the damp earth as she sprinted along the wooded path near the river. Her heart pounded against her ribs, fear clawing at her throat. She dared not look back—she knew someone was behind her. The sound of hurried footsteps echoed through the trees, quickening with every frantic step she took.

A figure emerged from the darkness, closing the distance between them. Emily tried to scream, but a gloved hand clamped over her mouth, muffling her cry. The force knocked her off balance, sending her sprawling onto the wet ground. The last thing she saw before everything went black was the shimmering reflection of the moon on the water.

The river swallowed her scream.

I

The Body in the River

Detective Daniel Mercer tightened his grip on the steering wheel as he maneuvered through the winding roads of Ridgewood. The town looked the same as it had years ago—quaint, quiet, and hiding secrets beneath its picturesque facade. The mist hung low over the streets, an unsettling shroud that did little to ease the weight pressing on his chest.

The call had come in early that morning. A jogger had spotted a body floating near the riverbank. By the time the local authorities arrived, the currents had pushed it against the rocks, as if the town itself had refused to let the dead go unnoticed.

Mercer parked near the flashing blue-and-red lights and stepped out, the damp air heavy with the scent of earth and decay. Sheriff Tom Wilkes, a grizzled man with deep lines etched into his face, greeted him with a nod.

"Bad one, Dan," Wilkes muttered, leading him toward the river. "Young girl. High school age. Looks like she'd been in the water a while."

Mercer crouched near the edge, his sharp eyes scanning the scene. Emily Carter's lifeless body lay half-submerged, her once-vibrant eyes staring blankly at the overcast sky. The water had done its work—her skin was pale, her lips tinged with blue, but the bruises around her wrists and neck told a different story.

This wasn't an accident. This was murder.

And Ridgewood had just become a hunting ground.

II

The Detective and the Past

Detective Mercer stood at the edge of the riverbank, the past creeping into his mind like an unwelcome ghost. Ridgewood wasn't just another case for him—it was a place he had sworn never to return to. But murder had a way of pulling people back to places they wanted to forget.

As the forensic team worked the crime scene, Mercer's mind drifted to another crime, years ago. His sister, Lydia, had vanished from this very town when she was just seventeen. They never found her body. The case had gone cold, much like Emily Carter's body now lying before him.

Wilkes cleared his throat beside him. "You okay, Dan?"

Mercer forced himself back to the present. "Yeah. Just thinking."

"I get it. This one feels... different. Something's off."

Mercer nodded, kneeling beside the medical examiner, Dr. Claire Reynolds, as she examined the girl's bruised wrists.

"Cause of death?" Mercer asked.

Claire sighed. "Preliminary guess—strangulation. But she has defensive wounds. She fought back. I'll know more after the autopsy."

Mercer's jaw tightened. The murderer hadn't just wanted Emily dead. They had made sure she suffered.

A uniformed officer approached, holding a clear evidence bag. "Detective, we found this near the brush, about twenty yards upstream."

Inside the bag was a delicate silver necklace, broken at the clasp. A single word was engraved on the pendant: Lydia.

Mercer felt his stomach drop. His past and present had just collided in the most chilling way possible.

III

A Town with Secrets

Ridgewood had always been a town that thrived on whispers. Behind every polite smile and friendly wave lay an unspoken truth—everyone had something to hide. Mercer knew this better than anyone.

Walking through the town square, he felt the weight of the residents' gazes. Some recognized him frts

ears ago, others simply saw the badge and knew why he was here. The death of a teenage girl would unsettle any community, but in Ridgewood, it felt like more than just fear. It felt like guilt.

Mercer stopped at Ridgewood High, the place where Emily Carter had spent most of her days. Principal Heather Lawson met him at the entrance, her face tight with concern.

"Detective Mercer, this is... awful," she said, shaking her head. "Emily was a bright girl. A little rebellious, but kind-hearted. She didn't deserve this."

"Did she have any problems? Anyone she was afraid of?" Mercer asked.

Lawson hesitated before answering. "She had a falling out with her best friend, Olivia Turner, recently. No one knew why. And... well, there was Ryan Hale, her boyfriend. Young love can be complicated."

Mercer made a mental note. A troubled friendship and a boyfriend—both worth looking into.

Just as he was about to leave, a student lingered near the lockers, watching him. When Mercer caught his eye, the boy quickly turned away.

"Who's that?" Mercer asked.

Lawson sighed. "That's Jack Dawson. He... keeps to himself. Had some trouble with the law before. People tend to blame him for things around here."

Mercer had learned long ago that towns like Ridgewood loved their scapegoats. But that didn't mean Jack Dawson was innocent.

Something told him this case was about to get even darker.

IV
Threads of Deception

Jack hesitated before speaking. "Look, I know how this looks. But I swear, I had nothing to do with Emily's death."

Mercer studied him closely. "Then tell me what you do know. Every detail matters."

Jack exhaled sharply and ran a hand through his dark hair. "Emily was... scared. She told me someone had been following her for weeks. She thought she was imagining things at first, but then she started getting these weird messages."

Mercer's eyes narrowed. "Messages? From who?"

Jack shook his head. "She never said. Just that they knew things about her—personal things. She didn't trust anyone, not even Olivia. That's why they had a falling out."

Mercer felt his pulse quicken. "And you didn't think to tell anyone?"

Jack scoffed. "You think anyone in this town listens to me? I've been blamed for every damn thing that goes wrong since I was thirteen. I tried to help her. I told her to go to the police, but she was too scared."

Mercer took a deep breath. There was more to Emily's murder than he had initially thought. And Jack Dawson, whether guilty or not, had just given him a crucial piece of the puzzle.

V
The Missing Witness

The morning sun barely broke through the thick fog as Mercer made his way to the town's diner. He had received a tip from an anonymous source claiming they had seen Emily the night before her murder. If true, this could be a game-changer.

The diner was nearly empty except for a waitress behind the counter and an older man nursing a black coffee. Mercer approached a booth where a nervous young woman sat, her fingers tracing the rim of a cold cup of tea.

"Detective Mercer?" she whispered.

He nodded and slid into the seat across from her. "You called the tip line?"

She glanced around before answering. "I saw Emily that night. She was scared. Said someone was following her."

Mercer leaned in. "Did she say who?"

"No... but she kept looking over her shoulder. She told me she was going to meet someone at the abandoned fairground."

Mercer's gut clenched. The fairground had been shut down for years. It was the perfect place for a secret meeting—or an ambush.

"You didn't tell anyone else?"

She shook her head. "I was afraid. But now... I think whoever killed her might have seen me, too."

Mercer's blood ran cold. "You're in danger. I need you to come with me."

As they stood, the bell above the diner's door jingled. A man in a dark hoodie entered, his eyes scanning the room before locking onto the woman. Her face went pale.

"That's him," she whispered.

Mercer reached for his gun. "Stay behind me."

The man hesitated for only a second before turning and bolting out the door. Mercer sprinted after him, heart pounding, as they burst into the morning fog. The chase was on.

The man dodged into an alleyway, his footsteps slapping against the wet pavement. Mercer pushed himself harder, his breath coming fast. He was closing in.

Suddenly, the suspect veered left, vaulting over a chain-link fence. Mercer scrambled after him, landing hard on the other side. The man twisted around, pulling a knife from his pocket.

"Stop! Police!" Mercer barked, leveling his gun.

The suspect hesitated, then lunged. Mercer dodged, the blade missing him by inches. He slammed the suspect against the wall, twisting the weapon from his grip.

"Talk!" Mercer growled, pinning him down. "Who are you? Why was Emily at the fairground?"

The man sneered. "You're too late, Detective. The truth died with her."

Mercer's grip tightened. "We'll see about that."

VI

A Killer's Game

The interrogation room was dimly lit, a single flickering bulb casting eerie shadows across the metal table. Detective Mercer leaned forward, his knuckles pressing into the cold surface. Across from him sat the suspect—the man who had fled the diner. His hoodie was damp with sweat, his hands twitching as he stared at the floor.

"You ran," Mercer said coolly. "Why?"

The man exhaled sharply. "Because I know what happens to people who talk."

Mercer crossed his arms. "Well, you're going to talk. Because right now, you're looking like the best lead I have. And if you're not the killer, you'd better start convincing me fast."

The man hesitated, licking his lips nervously. "I didn't kill her. I swear. But I know who did."

Mercer's heart pounded. "Who?"

The man glanced around as if the walls had ears. "Emily got mixed up in something bad. She found out something she wasn't supposed to, and they silenced her."

"Who's 'they'?" Mercer pressed.

"The people who run this town. The ones who make sure secrets stay buried."

Mercer frowned. "Give me a name."

The man hesitated before whispering, "Mayor Caldwell."

A tense silence filled the room. Mercer's gut clenched. If the mayor was involved, this case was far bigger than he had anticipated.

Before Mercer could press further, a loud bang echoed from the hallway. The door burst open, and an officer stumbled in, his face pale. "Detective, we have a situation."

Mercer shot to his feet. "What happened?"

"The witness—the girl from the diner. She's missing."

A chill ran down Mercer's spine. He turned back to the suspect, whose face had gone even paler. "They know she talked," he whispered. "She's as good as dead."

Mercer didn't waste another second. He grabbed his coat and bolted from the room. He had to find her before it was too late.

The streets of Ridgewood were eerily quiet as Mercer sped through the town, his mind racing. The girl had been terrified—she had known something crucial. And now she was gone.

His phone buzzed. It was Wilkes. "Mercer, we got a lead. A car matching the suspect's description was seen heading toward the old Carter farm."

Mercer gripped the wheel. "I'm on my way."

The Carter farm had been abandoned for years, ever since Emily's family moved away. If the witness had been taken there, it wasn't for a friendly chat.

As Mercer neared the property, he killed his headlights, pulling up a few yards away. The farmhouse loomed ahead, its windows dark, its structure rotting with age. A single car was parked outside.

Mercer checked his gun before stepping out of his vehicle. He moved silently, pressing himself against the side of the house, listening. Muffled voices came from inside.

He crept to a window and peered through a crack in the wooden planks. Two men stood over the girl, who was tied to a chair, her eyes wide with terror.

"You should've kept your mouth shut," one of them growled.

Mercer didn't hesitate. He slammed his shoulder into the door, sending it flying open. The men spun around, but Mercer had his gun trained on them.

"Ridgewood PD! Hands in the air!"

One of the men reached for something in his jacket, but Mercer fired a warning shot into the floor. "I said hands up!"

They complied, but the girl was trembling. "Detective… they were going to kill me."

Mercer nodded. "Not on my watch."

He radioed for backup, keeping his weapon steady. He wasn't taking any chances. This case had just taken a dangerous turn, and he was more determined than ever to uncover the truth.

VII

The Confession That Wasn't

Detective Mercer stood outside the Ridgewood Police Station, staring up at the darkened sky. The events of the night weighed heavily on his shoulders. He had rescued the witness, but he knew this was just the beginning. The conspiracy stretched far deeper than he had anticipated, and now, the name Mayor Caldwell loomed over everything like a shadow.

Inside, the two men arrested at the Carter farm sat in separate interrogation rooms, each refusing to speak without legal representation. Mercer wasn't concerned. He had time. But time wasn't on the side of the missing pieces in this puzzle. He needed answers—fast.

Wilkes stepped up beside him. "We have one of them willing to talk," he said. "The younger guy—Mark Evans. He's rattled."

Mercer nodded. "Let's break him."

Interrogation Room 2

Mark Evans sat with his hands cuffed in front of him, sweat glistening on his forehead. Mercer pulled up a chair across from him and set down a file folder, slowly flipping it open to reveal photos of Emily Carter's body. Evans looked away, his Adam's apple bobbing.

"I didn't sign up for this," Evans muttered, his voice barely above a whisper.

"Didn't sign up for what?" Mercer leaned forward. "Murder? Cover-ups? You tell me, Mark. Because right now, you're an accessory. And I don't think you're the type who enjoys prison food."

Evans shuddered. "I just did what I was told."

"Told by who?" Mercer pressed.

Evans hesitated, his fingers twitching against the table. "It wasn't supposed to go this far," he admitted. "We were supposed to scare her. Just scare her into keeping quiet."

Mercer clenched his jaw. "Who gave the order?"

Evans swallowed hard. "Mayor Caldwell. But he's not the one running things."

Mercer's grip on his pen tightened. "Then who is?"

"I don't know their real name. Everyone just calls him The Architect. He's the one pulling the strings in this town."

Mercer's stomach turned. A shadowy figure behind it all—a mastermind orchestrating the corruption and murder in Ridgewood. He needed more than a nickname.

"Where do I find him?"

Evans shook his head. "Nobody meets him directly. Caldwell takes orders from him. The only way to get to The Architect is through Caldwell."

Mercer stood, pacing the room. This was bigger than he had thought. Emily Carter had stumbled upon something much darker than a simple crime. She had unearthed a conspiracy that had its grip on the town's highest powers.

The Mayor's Alibi

Later that evening, Mercer and Wilkes arrived at the mayor's estate. The grand, historic house was adorned with tall iron gates and security cameras. Mercer doubted Caldwell would go down without a fight.

A butler opened the door, eyeing them with disdain. "The mayor is expecting you," he said before leading them inside.

Caldwell sat in his lavish study, swirling a glass of whiskey. He looked up with a smug smile. "Detective Mercer. To what do I owe the pleasure?"

"We have a witness linking you to Emily Carter's death," Mercer said, cutting straight to the point.

Caldwell chuckled, setting his glass down. "A witness? Interesting. Because I was at a charity gala that night, surrounded by dozens of people. Care to check the guest list?"

Mercer's patience thinned. "You don't need to get your hands dirty when you have people like Mark Evans doing it for you."

Caldwell's smile faltered. "You're grasping at straws, detective. You have no proof. Just the words of a scared young man."

Mercer stepped closer, placing both hands on the desk. "And what about The Architect? Care to explain who that is?"

Caldwell's eyes darkened for the first time. "You should stop digging, Mercer. Some truths are buried for a reason."

Mercer didn't flinch. "I don't stop. I dig until I find the truth. And you're running out of places to hide."

Caldwell leaned back, his smirk returning. "Then I guess we'll see who finds what first."

Mercer turned on his heel, exiting the room. He had no doubt now—Mayor Caldwell wasn't just involved. He was protecting someone. And if that someone was The Architect, then the real game was just beginning.

A Deadly Message

As Mercer drove back to the station, his phone buzzed. An unknown number. He answered cautiously. "Mercer."

A distorted voice crackled through the speaker. "You should have left this alone, detective."

Mercer gritted his teeth. "Who is this?"

A low chuckle. "A warning. Walk away, or you won't live to see the truth."

The line went dead.

Mercer's grip tightened on the wheel. The hunt for The Architect had officially begun.

VIII

Truth Beneath the Lies

Detective Mercer sat in his office, staring at the pile of evidence spread out before him. The pieces were beginning to connect, but the full picture remained elusive. Mayor Caldwell was involved, that much was clear. But *The Architect*—the shadowy figure pulling the strings—was still just a name, a ghost hidden within Ridgewood's darkest corners.

A knock on the door broke his concentration. Wilkes stepped in, his face grim. "We have another body, Dan."

Mercer's heart sank. "Who?"

Wilkes hesitated before answering. "Mark Evans."

Mercer shot to his feet. "The guy from interrogation?"

Wilkes nodded. "Found in his holding cell this morning. Hanged himself—or at least, that's what they want us to believe."

Mercer grabbed his coat. "Let's go."

The Crime Scene

The holding cells at Ridgewood PD were eerily quiet. Evans' body dangled from a bedsheet tied to the bars, his face contorted in agony. Mercer took in the details—no signs of struggle, no defensive wounds. Too clean. Too precise.

"This wasn't suicide," Mercer muttered. "This was a message."

Wilkes exhaled sharply. "From *The Architect?*"

"Or someone cleaning up his mess," Mercer replied. "Either way, it tells us one thing—whoever's behind this is getting nervous."

Mercer crouched beside the body, examining Evans' hands. Beneath his fingernails, faint traces of ink. A note, hastily written before his death.

Wilkes handed him a pair of gloves. "Think he left us something?"

Carefully, Mercer pried open Evans' clenched fist. A crumpled scrap of paper slipped out. Three words were scrawled in shaky handwriting:

Warehouse. Midnight. Alone.

Mercer's jaw tightened. "Looks like he tried to give us a lead before they got to him."

Wilkes frowned. "You're not seriously thinking about going, are you? It's obviously a trap."

"Of course, it's a trap," Mercer said, pocketing the note. "But it's the only one we've got."

Into the Shadows

Midnight came faster than Mercer had anticipated. He sat in his car, parked outside an abandoned warehouse on the outskirts of Ridgewood. The place was decrepit, its windows shattered, its structure barely holding together.

He checked his gun before stepping out, every instinct screaming at him to turn back. But he couldn't. Not now.

Inside, the air was thick with dust and decay. Mercer moved cautiously, his flashlight slicing through the darkness. The faint sound of footsteps echoed somewhere in the distance.

"You came alone. Good."

Mercer spun around, gun raised. A figure emerged from the shadows—a man in a tailored suit, his face partially obscured by the dim light.

"Who are you?" Mercer demanded.

The man smirked. "You already know."

Mercer's pulse quickened. "*The Architect.*"

The man gave a slow nod. "I expected you to be smarter, Mercer. Getting this close to the truth—dangerous game."

Mercer's grip tightened on his gun. "You killed Emily Carter. You killed Mark Evans. How many more bodies before you get what you want?"

The Architect chuckled. "Emily wasn't supposed to die. She was warned. She didn't listen. That made her a liability."

"And what about Evans?"

"He knew too much. He talked. Loose ends get tied up."

Mercer's blood boiled. "You're going to pay for this."

The smirk faded from *The Architect's* face. "No, detective. You will."

The sound of a gun cocking behind him sent Mercer's stomach into freefall.

"Drop it," a voice ordered.

Slowly, Mercer raised his hands, his own weapon clattering to the ground. The trap had been set, and he had walked straight into it.

The Architect sighed. "A shame, really. You were getting close. Too close. But this is where your story ends."

A shot rang out.

Mercer flinched—but the bullet wasn't meant for him.

The Architect stumbled back, clutching his shoulder, blood seeping through his pristine suit. Behind him, Wilkes stood, gun smoking, eyes blazing with determination.

"You really thought I'd let you go alone?" Wilkes said, stepping forward.

Mercer wasted no time. He grabbed his gun, levelling it at *The Architect* as the man staggered against a pillar.

"You're under arrest," Mercer said coldly. "It's over."

The Architect chuckled weakly, blood dripping from his lips. "You still don't get it, do you? This isn't over. This is just the beginning."

Wilkes cuffed him as backup swarmed the warehouse. Mercer exhaled, his hands shaking slightly. He had won this round—but he had a feeling *The Architect* wasn't lying.

Something bigger was coming.

And he had just scratched the surface.

IX

The Final Hunt

Detective Mercer stood outside the Ridgewood Police Department, staring into the dark horizon. The events of the past few days had unravelled a conspiracy far deeper than he had imagined. *The Architect* was in custody, but Mercer knew this wasn't over. There were more players in the game, more secrets buried beneath Ridgewood's picturesque facade.

Wilkes approached him, hands in his pockets. "For a man who just took down one of the biggest criminals in town, you don't look too thrilled."

Mercer exhaled. "Because this isn't over."

Wilkes nodded. "We got a call an hour ago. Anonymous tip. There's an old farmhouse on the outskirts of town—apparently, it's where *The Architect* conducted business. If there's more evidence, that's where we'll find it."

Mercer checked his watch. "Then we don't waste any time. Let's move."

The Farmhouse

The road to the farmhouse was long and deserted, surrounded by nothing but mist-covered fields. Mercer's fingers tightened around the steering wheel. The deeper they dug, the more dangerous this case became.

Wilkes cocked his shotgun as they stepped out of the car. "Place looks abandoned."

Mercer scanned the property. The farmhouse stood in eerie silence, its windows boarded up, its structure worn from years of neglect. But something felt off. "Stay sharp. We don't know what we're walking into."

As they approached the door, Mercer noticed faint tire tracks in the dirt, fresh ones. Someone had been here recently.

Wilkes signalled to the back while Mercer took point at the front door. With one swift kick, the door burst open, revealing a dimly lit interior cluttered with old furniture and stacks of documents. A single lamp flickered on a table in the centre of the room.

"Looks like someone left in a hurry," Wilkes muttered, shuffling through the papers.

Mercer's eyes landed on a map pinned to the wall, covered in red markings. Ridgewood's major landmarks were circled—City Hall, the police station, the high school. And beneath the map, a name scribbled hastily: *Mercer.*

His blood ran cold. "They were tracking us."

A noise from the second floor made both men freeze.

Wilkes raised his shotgun. "We're not alone."

The Chase

The creak of floorboards above sent Mercer into motion. He bolted up the stairs, gun drawn, heart pounding in his chest. A shadow darted down the hallway.

"Stop! Ridgewood PD!" Mercer yelled.

The figure didn't stop. Instead, it crashed through a side window, landing hard in the overgrown grass below. Mercer didn't hesitate—he followed, the night air stinging against his skin as he hit the ground running.

Wilkes shouted from behind. "I'll cut them off!"

The suspect was fast, but Mercer was faster. He tackled the figure to the ground, pinning them beneath him. The person struggled, but Mercer pressed his gun to their temple.

"Who sent you?"

The hooded figure stilled; their breath ragged. Then, a raspy voice murmured, "You don't know what you've done, detective."

Mercer yanked the hood back—his stomach lurched. It was a teenage boy, no older than seventeen, terror in his wide eyes.

"Who are you working for?" Mercer demanded.

The boy shook his head. "It's too late. He's already gone."

Mercer's grip tightened. "Who?"

A slow smile crept across the boy's face. "*The Architect* was just the beginning. You have no idea how deep this goes."

Before Mercer could respond, a single gunshot rang out. The boy gasped, his body jerking beneath Mercer's hold. Blood pooled beneath his chest.

Mercer's head snapped up. In the distance, a shadowy figure stood on the ridge, a rifle aimed in his direction. Then, just as quickly as they had appeared, they vanished into the fog.

"Wilkes!" Mercer called. "We have a shooter!"

Wilkes ran up, eyes darting around. "Damn it, they got him."

Mercer pressed a hand against the boy's wound, but it was useless. His breathing slowed, and within seconds, he was gone.

"Damn it!" Mercer slammed his fist into the ground. They had been so close. Someone was still pulling the strings, and now another lead was dead.

Wilkes pulled him up. "We need to move. They won't stop until this case is buried for good."

Mercer's jaw tightened. "Then we dig deeper. Because I'm not stopping until I bring every last one of them down."

The night stretched endlessly before them; the fog thick with danger. Mercer had uncovered a secret war, and Ridgewood was the battlefield.

And this was far from over.

X

Justice in the Dark

Mercer stood in his office, staring at the evidence board covered in photos, maps, and notes connected with red string. Ridgewood's conspiracy had claimed too many lives, but now, Mercer was closer than ever to the truth. He had uncovered *The Architect*, but the web of corruption stretched further, deeper, beyond what he had imagined. The final piece of the puzzle lay just out of reach.

Wilkes entered, dropping a file onto Mercer's desk. "Forensics analyzed the farmhouse documents. You were right. There's another name linked to all of this."

Mercer flipped open the file. His eyes darkened. *Senator William Kane.*

"A senator?" Mercer muttered. "That explains the resources, the reach... but what's his connection to Ridgewood?"

Wilkes crossed his arms. "He's been funding projects in town for years. But there's more—phone records show direct calls between Kane and *The Architect* over the past six months. Whatever they were planning, it involved more than just Ridgewood."

Mercer exhaled. "Then it's time we paid Kane a visit."

The Confrontation

Senator Kane's estate was a fortress—high walls, security cameras, private guards. Mercer and Wilkes knew they wouldn't get in the easy way. They waited until nightfall before making their move, slipping through the dense woods surrounding the property.

"We should have backup," Wilkes whispered.

"No time," Mercer said. "If we wait, he'll bury the evidence. We go in now."

They scaled the fence, landing in the shadows of a manicured garden. Lights illuminated the mansion's back patio, and through the large windows, they saw Kane—seated in a leather chair, sipping a glass of bourbon, completely at ease.

Mercer crept forward, gun drawn. They entered through an unlocked side door, moving silently through the darkened halls.

Then, a voice rang out. "I was wondering when you'd show up, Detective."

Kane stood at the end of the corridor, flanked by two armed guards. He smirked. "You've been a thorn in my side for too long."

Mercer stepped forward, keeping his gun steady. "Emily Carter. Mark Evans. The Architect. How many more people have to die before this ends?"

Kane sighed, shaking his head. "You don't understand, Mercer. Ridgewood is just the beginning. Corruption isn't a disease—it's the foundation of power. You can't stop this."

"We'll see about that," Mercer said.

The guards raised their weapons. The room erupted into chaos.

The Fight for Survival

Gunfire echoed through the mansion as Mercer and Wilkes dove for cover. Wilkes fired first, taking down one of Kane's men, while Mercer rolled behind a marble column, returning fire. The second guard fell, leaving Kane scrambling for an escape.

"He's running!" Wilkes shouted.

Mercer pursued Kane through the halls, his footsteps pounding against polished floors. Kane burst through a hidden door, leading into an underground tunnel.

"Damn it!" Mercer cursed, following him into the darkness.

The tunnel stretched deep beneath the estate, lined with old stone and flickering lights. Kane had the advantage—he knew the layout. Mercer pushed forward, his breath ragged.

Ahead, Kane reached a locked steel door. He fumbled for a keycard, but Mercer was faster. He tackled the senator to the ground, pinning him.

"It's over!" Mercer growled.

Kane struggled. "You have no idea what you're interfering with! There are people above me—far worse than you can imagine!"

Mercer pressed his knee into Kane's back. "Then start talking."

The Final Revelation

Kane laughed, a chilling sound in the confined space. "You think arresting me will change anything? The people I answer to—they'll erase everything. Including you."

Wilkes caught up, cuffs in hand. "We'll take our chances."

Kane sneered. "Then you're both already dead men."

As they hauled Kane to his feet, Mercer's phone buzzed. A message flashed across the screen:

You can't stop what's coming.

A chill ran through Mercer. This wasn't just about Ridgewood anymore. The fight had only just begun.

Shadows Remain

Weeks later, Kane's arrest sent shockwaves through the political world. Evidence of corruption surfaced, but as Mercer had feared, some files disappeared, and key witnesses vanished. Ridgewood had seen justice—for now. But Mercer knew the truth. He had only uncovered the tip of the iceberg.

As he stood at Emily Carter's grave, he made a silent promise.

He wasn't done yet.

And neither were they.

XI

A New Case Begins

The town of Ridgewood had barely recovered from the revelations of corruption and conspiracy when another chilling crime rocked its quiet streets. Detective Daniel Mercer sat at his desk, reviewing the files from the Kane case, when his phone buzzed. He answered without looking. "Mercer."

"Detective, you need to see this," Wilkes' voice was grave. "We've got a body—downtown. And it's not just any body."

Mercer grabbed his coat. "I'm on my way."

The Crime Scene

The alley was narrow, the air thick with the scent of decay and something worse—something metallic. Blood pooled beneath the victim, forming a crimson halo on the cold pavement. The body, a middle-aged man, lay sprawled against a dumpster, his throat slashed cleanly, surgically. His eyes were still open, frozen in terror. A light drizzle fell from the sky, adding a sheen to the blood-soaked ground. A single flickering streetlight cast long, ominous shadows across the scene.

Wilkes stood nearby, rubbing his chin. "No ID. No phone. Just this."

He handed Mercer a small, blood-stained card. On it, a single phrase was printed:

Did you think it was over?

Mercer's grip tightened. "They're taunting us."

Wilkes exhaled. "And they just started a new game."

Mercer scanned the area. The alley had no security cameras, no obvious witnesses. Whoever did this had planned it meticulously. He crouched beside the body, inspecting the wound. "This cut—it's not just precise, it's surgical. Whoever did this knew anatomy."

Wilkes looked uneasy. "A doctor? A butcher? Someone trained?"

Mercer nodded grimly. "Possibly military or medical background. Either way, this wasn't random."

The Investigation Begins

Back at the station, the coroner, Dr. Claire Reynolds, examined the body. "Whoever did this knew what they were doing. The cut was precise, severing the carotid instantly. No hesitation. No jagged edges."

Mercer leaned over the examination table. "A professional. But why leave a message? Why make this personal?"

Reynolds pulled back the victim's sleeve. A tattoo was inked onto his wrist—a symbol Mercer recognized from one of the case files in Kane's network. A circular design with an intricate pattern, one he had seen before.

Wilkes noticed Mercer's expression. "What is it?"

Mercer sighed. "This isn't just a random killing. This man was connected to Kane."

Wilkes shook his head. "Then this isn't over."

Mercer nodded grimly. "Not by a long shot."

Reynolds peeled off her gloves. "There's something else. The victim had defensive wounds, but they're odd. Almost ritualistic. Shallow cuts along his palms. It's like the killer wanted to send a message."

Mercer frowned. "A warning? Or an initiation?"

Wilkes ran a hand through his hair. "Mercer, if this is tied to Kane's network, then we're looking at something much bigger than a simple revenge killing."

Mercer stared at the corpse, his gut tightening. "Then we start digging. Whoever left that card wants us to play their game. Let's find out what the rules are."

XII

A Killer's Calling Card

Detective Daniel Mercer sat in the dimly lit interrogation room, staring at the evidence board cluttered with photographs, newspaper clippings, and crime scene reports. The latest murder was unlike the others. It was deliberate. It was staged. And it was meant for him.

The small desk lamp cast long shadows across the walls, illuminating only the jagged edges of old case files and red string crisscrossing between key suspects. The air in the room was thick, a mixture of stale coffee and something else—something darker. The weight of the case pressed down on him like an iron fist.

A knock at the door pulled him from his thoughts. Wilkes entered, a thick folder in hand. "You're going to want to see this."

Mercer took the file, flipping it open. Inside were crime scene photos of another victim—same surgical precision, same eerie calmness in the corpse's expression. And beside the body, placed with an almost reverent care, was an old pocket watch, its hands frozen at exactly 3:33 AM.

"This was found next to the body?" Mercer asked, frowning.

Wilkes nodded grimly. "Same as the last one. We ran prints, but nothing. No ID on the victim either."

Mercer studied the pocket watch, running a gloved finger over its worn surface. "This is a signature. The killer wants us to know it's them."

"A calling card?" Wilkes asked.

"More than that," Mercer muttered. "It's a challenge. They're inviting us to play their game."

Wilkes exhaled. "Well, I hate games."

The Victim's Story

The body belonged to Thomas Gellar, a local journalist known for covering corruption cases. His apartment was an extension of his obsession—cluttered with stacks of old newspapers, case files pinned to the walls, and a corkboard littered with scribbled notes connected by frayed string.

The air inside was stale, a mix of ink, old paper, and cigarette smoke that had seeped into the furniture over time. The dim glow from an old desk lamp flickered against the peeling wallpaper, casting long, wavering shadows. A laptop sat open on the desk, the screen glowing with an unfinished article.

Wilkes ran a hand through his graying hair. "Looks like he was working on something big."

Mercer leaned in, reading aloud: "'The hidden players behind Ridgewood's darkest secrets... an organized network that goes deeper than anyone realizes...'"

Wilkes whistled. "Sounds like he got too close to something."

Mercer nodded. "And now he's dead."

There was a rustling sound from the hallway. Mercer and Wilkes exchanged glances before Mercer grabbed his gun. He moved silently toward the door, easing it open. The corridor was empty, but a single piece of paper had been slid under the door.

He bent down, picking it up. It was a printed note with a single line: **"Stay out of the dark."**

Wilkes stiffened. "You think someone was watching us?"

Mercer's jaw tightened. "I think someone still is."

The Message Behind the Murders

Back at the station, Mercer examined the evidence again. Two victims, both tied to uncovering secrets. Both murdered in the same meticulous fashion. The pocket watches. The cryptic message on the first body. Now, the warning note.

"This isn't random," Mercer said. "It's calculated. The killer is choosing people who threaten their operation."

Wilkes crossed his arms. "So, what now?"

Mercer exhaled, staring at the evidence board. "Now, we figure out who they're protecting. And who's next on their list."

Reynolds, the coroner, entered with a folder in hand. "You two might want to hear this. I ran additional tox screens on both victims."

Mercer raised an eyebrow. "And?"

She handed him the report. "They were both drugged before they were killed. A rare compound, something designed to paralyze without killing. It's not something you find on the street. This was specialized. Military-grade."

Wilkes frowned. "That means our killer has access to things normal people don't."

Mercer's mind raced. "Which means they're either in law enforcement, government... or worse."

Wilkes looked grim. "A trained killer covering up something big. That's bad, Mercer. Real bad."

XIII

A Trail of Ghosts

Detective Daniel Mercer hadn't slept in two days. His office was a mess of files, crime scene photos, and empty coffee cups. The eerie glow from his desk lamp cast long shadows on the walls, the only light breaking the dimness of the night. Outside, rain drizzled against the window, tapping like impatient fingers demanding answers.

Wilkes entered without knocking, his face drawn with exhaustion. "Tell me you've got something."

Mercer exhaled, rubbing his temples. "Gellar's last article—it wasn't just about Kane's corruption. It mentioned a name we've seen before."

Wilkes raised an eyebrow. "Don't keep me waiting."

Mercer slid a document across the desk. "Adrian Langley. Former Ridgewood PD. Dismissed from the force ten years ago. Gellar was investigating his disappearance."

Wilkes frowned. "Langley? Didn't he vanish without a trace?"

Mercer nodded. "And now two people tied to his name are dead. Someone didn't want Gellar digging into it. And now we have bodies piling up."

Wilkes ran a hand over his face. "Jesus, Mercer. What are we looking at here?"

Mercer leaned forward; eyes sharp. "A ghost. A cop turned into a phantom. And I think he's back."

A Visit to the Forgotten

Langley's last known address was a derelict house on the outskirts of Ridgewood, hidden behind a wall of overgrown brush and rusting chain-link fences. The place looked abandoned, but Mercer knew better. Places like this always held secrets, even when no one was left to tell them.

Wilkes pulled his jacket tighter against the cold. "Why do I feel like this is a bad idea?"

Mercer pushed open the rotting wooden gate. "Because it probably is."

Inside, the air was stale, thick with dust and decay. The wallpaper peeled in long strips, revealing crumbling drywall, its surface marred by sprawling veins of black mold, creeping like a sickness through the decaying wood and plaster, giving the entire space the feeling of something rotting from the inside out. Furniture sat untouched, coated in years of neglect. Yet something felt off—an unnatural stillness, like someone had been here recently.

Mercer's eyes swept the room, landing on a small table in the corner. A single candle sat in the center, melted wax pooling at its base. "Someone's been here."

Wilkes muttered a curse under his breath. "You thinking what I'm thinking?"

Mercer knelt beside the table, running his fingers over the wax. "Not just thinking it. I know it. Langley was here."

A creak echoed from the back of the house. Both detectives froze. Mercer's hand went to his gun. Wilkes pulled his own weapon, eyes scanning the darkness beyond the hallway.

Then, a whisper.

Mercer's breath caught. It was faint, barely audible, but it was there.

Leave.

Wilkes turned toward him; eyes wide. "Tell me you heard that."

Mercer nodded, his pulse hammering. "Yeah. I heard it."

A Message from the Past

They didn't find anyone in the house, but Mercer's gut told him they weren't alone. The next morning, a manila envelope was waiting on his desk at the station. No return address. Just his name, written in block letters.

Wilkes hovered over his shoulder as he opened it. Inside was a single photograph—grainy, black and white, clearly taken from a distance. It showed Adrian Langley standing in an alleyway, looking directly at the camera.

Wilkes swore. "That's recent."

Mercer turned the photo over. A single word was scrawled on the back in uneven ink:

Stop.

Mercer tightened his grip on the paper. "Looks like Langley doesn't want to be found."

Wilkes let out a humourless laugh. "Yeah, well, he just made damn sure we'll find him."

Mercer studied the photo again. "Langley is hunting something. And if we don't get to him first... we might be the next names on his list."

XIV

The Hunter and the Hunted

The rain came down in thick sheets, drumming against the windshield of Mercer's car as he sat parked in a deserted lot overlooking the city. The glow of the streetlights shimmered in the puddles on the cracked asphalt, distorting their reflection like a funhouse mirror. Inside the car, the air was thick with tension.

Wilkes sat in the passenger seat, flipping through the file on Adrian Langley. "This guy was a damn good cop before he disappeared. Commendations, undercover work—then one day, poof. No official record of why he left the force, no disciplinary action, nothing. Just vanished."

Mercer tapped a finger against the wheel. "Someone wanted him erased. Question is, why is he resurfacing now?"

Wilkes glanced at him. "You think he's behind the killings?"

Mercer exhaled. "I don't know yet. But he's definitely connected. The question is whether he's the predator or the prey."

A buzz from Mercer's phone broke the silence. An anonymous message flashed on the screen:

Meet me at Pier 17. Midnight. Come alone.

Wilkes frowned. "That can't be good."

Mercer started the engine. "Only one way to find out."

A Meeting in the Dark

The pier was nearly abandoned at this hour, save for the occasional vagrant huddled under the skeletal remains of an old boathouse. The water lapped lazily against the wooden pilings, a rhythmic, hollow sound beneath the steady hum of the city in the distance.

Mercer stepped out of his car, his coat pulled tight against the wind. His hand rested on his holster as he scanned the shadows. A figure emerged from the darkness, moving with a slow, deliberate confidence.

Adrian Langley.

Mercer didn't raise his weapon, but he didn't relax either. "You've been leaving messages."

Langley stopped a few feet away, his face partially obscured by the hood of his jacket. "I needed to see if you were as smart as they say."

Mercer's eyes narrowed. "Who's 'they'? The people you ran from? The people who want you dead?"

Langley exhaled, the mist of his breath curling in the cold air. "You don't know what you're dealing with, detective. The bodies you've found? They're just the beginning."

Mercer took a step closer. "Then start talking."

Langley smirked, but there was no humor in it. "You ever wonder why Kane was so untouchable? Why every lead in his case hit a dead end until it was too late?" He leaned in, voice barely above a whisper. "Because he wasn't the top of the chain. There's someone bigger. Someone who's been pulling the strings in Ridgewood for decades."

Mercer felt a familiar chill creep up his spine. "Give me a name."

Langley shook his head. "You don't want a name, Mercer. You want proof. And I can give it to you. But not here. Not yet."

A sharp noise—a footstep on gravel. Both men turned, but the shadows remained still. Langley tensed. "You brought someone?"

Mercer shook his head. "No. But it looks like we're not alone."

Before Mercer could react, a gunshot rang out.

Langley jerked, stumbling back, a dark stain blossoming across his shoulder. "Damn it!" he hissed, clutching the wound.

Mercer spun, drawing his gun, but the shooter had already vanished into the night.

Langley staggered but caught himself. "This is what I was talking about. They don't care who sees. They don't leave loose ends."

Mercer grabbed his arm. "We need to get you somewhere safe. Now."

Langley shook his head. "No hospitals. No cops. They'll find me there."

Mercer swore under his breath. "Then where?"

Langley's expression was grim. "There's an old safe house. You want answers? That's where we go. But we have to move now."

Mercer hesitated only a moment before nodding. "Then let's go."

Wilkes was going to kill him.

The Safe House

Langley's 'safe house' was an abandoned warehouse on the outskirts of town. The inside smelled of oil and rust, long-forgotten tools scattered across workbenches covered in dust. The only light came from a single exposed bulb hanging from the ceiling.

Mercer helped Langley onto a crate, tearing open a first-aid kit. "You going to tell me what the hell is going on now?"

Langley winced as Mercer pressed gauze to his wound. "I used to be one of them. The people running Ridgewood from the shadows. I thought I could change things from the inside. I was wrong."

Mercer's hand stilled. "How deep does it go?"

Langley's gaze was hollow. "Deeper than you want to know. You think Kane was the worst of it? He was a puppet. The real power—the people I worked for—they don't have names. Just influence."

Mercer felt his jaw tighten. "And they sent someone to kill you tonight."

Langley nodded. "They know I've been watching. And now they know you have, too."

Mercer sat back, rubbing his temples. "So what do we do?"

Langley managed a weak smile. "We take the fight to them."

Wilkes' voice crackled over Mercer's radio, tense. "Mercer, where the hell are you? We got another body. And this one? It's personal."

Mercer and Langley locked eyes.
The game had just changed.

XV

Blood in the Shadows

The phone call had been brief—tense, clipped words from Wilkes that barely concealed the urgency behind them. "Mercer, you need to get down here. Now."

Mercer gripped the steering wheel as he sped through the rain-slicked streets of Ridgewood, his gut twisting with unease. Wilkes wasn't the type to sound rattled. If he did, it meant something had gone terribly wrong.

When Mercer pulled up to the scene, he barely had time to cut the engine before Wilkes was at his window, face pale under the flashing red-and-blue lights. "It's bad, Dan. Real bad."

Mercer stepped out, the cold wind biting through his jacket as he followed Wilkes past the police barricade. The alleyway was drenched in rain and blood. A body lay sprawled against the brick wall, the chest carved open in deliberate, jagged strokes. The scent of iron mixed with damp asphalt filled the air.

Claire Reynolds, the coroner, knelt beside the corpse, her expression grim. "Whoever did this wanted to send a message."

Mercer crouched down, eyes scanning the body. Then he froze.

The victim wasn't just anyone.

It was Officer Mark Davison—one of their own.

A Message in Blood

"Goddamn it," Wilkes muttered, running a hand through his soaked hair. "This isn't just a murder. It's a goddamn declaration."

Mercer's jaw clenched. "And it's personal."

Claire lifted a gloved hand, revealing something clutched in Davison's fingers. A piece of paper, soaked in blood, but the words scrawled across it were still visible.

He saw too much.

Mercer took the note, his grip tightening. "Langley warned me this was bigger than Kane. This proves it. Someone is tying up loose ends."

Wilkes shook his head. "Then we need to figure out what Davison knew—and fast."

The Break-In

Mercer and Wilkes wasted no time getting to Davison's apartment. The door was ajar, the lock shattered. Mercer drew his gun, motioning for Wilkes to stay close. The air inside was still, heavy with the scent of overturned whiskey and paper burned in haste.

Wilkes moved toward the desk, brushing aside ashes. "They tried to destroy something."

Mercer knelt, sifting through half-burned papers. One fragment caught his eye. A list of names.

And his own was on it.

Wilkes looked over his shoulder. "What the hell is this?"

"A hit list," Mercer muttered. "And I think we're next."

The Chase

A floorboard creaked.

Mercer barely had time to register the sound before a shadow lunged from the darkness. A figure in black crashed into him, sending them both sprawling. Mercer rolled, kicking up, but his attacker was fast, knife flashing in the dim light.

Wilkes fired a shot, but the figure ducked, shattering the window before vaulting onto the fire escape.

"Go!" Mercer barked, already sprinting after the fleeing silhouette.

The chase spilled onto the rain-slicked streets, Mercer's breath burning in his chest as he closed the gap. The figure darted into an abandoned construction site, the skeletal remains of an unfinished building looming ahead.

Mercer followed, heart pounding. The attacker disappeared into the shadows, but Mercer could feel them—watching. Waiting.

A whisper echoed through the empty space. "You should have stopped digging."

Mercer spun; gun raised. "Come out and face me."

Silence.

Then, a blade flashed.

Mercer barely dodged in time, the knife slicing past his ribs. He fired, but the attacker was already gone, footsteps fading into the night.

Wilkes arrived, breathless. "You get a look at them?"

Mercer's jaw clenched as he clutched his bleeding side. "No. But they knew me. And they wanted me dead."

Wilkes exhaled, eyes scanning the darkness. "We need to end this, Dan. Before they do."

Mercer wiped the blood from his fingers, eyes cold. "Then we find out who's pulling the strings. And we cut them down."

XVI

No Safe Haven

Mercer's shoulder throbbed from the close call with the knife, but adrenaline kept him upright. The attacker had vanished into the night, leaving behind only the echo of his whispered threat. Mercer knew one thing—whoever was behind this had grown bolder, and now, they wanted him out of the way.

Wilkes took one look at Mercer's wound and shook his head. "You need to get that looked at."

"Later," Mercer muttered, already dialling a number on his phone. It rang twice before a voice answered.

"Detective Mercer. I was expecting your call."

Mercer stiffened. "Langley."

Langley chuckled dryly. "You're finally starting to see, aren't you? They're everywhere. They know your every move. They won't stop until they bury every last trace of the truth."

"Then let's make sure they don't," Mercer growled. "I need to meet. Now."

Langley hesitated. "That's risky. They're watching me too. But I know a place."

The Safehouse

The location Langley provided was a run-down motel on the outskirts of Ridgewood, the kind of place where people disappeared without a trace. The neon 'VACANCY' sign flickered weakly, barely cutting through the thick fog rolling in from the hills.

Mercer parked a few rooms down and scanned the area. A few drifters loitered by the stairwell, but no immediate threats. Still, he kept his hand near his gun as he made his way to Room 104.

He knocked once.

The door creaked open, and Langley stood there, pistol in hand. His face was drawn, shadows clinging beneath his eyes. "You weren't followed?"

Mercer pushed past him into the room. "If I was, we'll know soon enough."

Langley shut the door and locked it. "You're in deep, Mercer. Deeper than you realize. Davison's murder? That was a warning. They're making their move."

Mercer leaned against the rickety table. "Then tell me what I'm missing. Who are they protecting? Who's calling the shots?"

Langley hesitated, then walked over to a duffel bag by the bed. He unzipped it, revealing stacks of documents, photos, and—most chilling of all—a file with Mercer's own name on it.

"You're on their list, Mercer. Have been for a while."

Mercer flipped open the file. Surveillance photos of him outside the station, in his apartment, even at his sister's grave. His blood ran cold. "They've been watching me this whole time."

Langley nodded. "And they won't stop. Not until you're in a body bag."

A Deadly Trap

Before Mercer could respond, the sound of tires screeching outside made both men tense. Langley moved to the window, pulling back the curtain just enough to peek outside. His breath caught. "Damn it."

Mercer grabbed his gun. "What?"

Langley turned; eyes sharp with urgency. "They found us."

Headlights beamed through the thin motel curtains as two black SUVs pulled up outside. Doors flew open, and masked figures in tactical gear poured out, weapons drawn.

"We're not making it out the front," Langley muttered, already moving toward the bathroom window. "Follow me."

Mercer didn't hesitate. As the first gunshots shattered the motel windows, he ducked, rolling behind the bed for cover.

Langley wrenched open the small window and hoisted himself through. "Move!"

Mercer fired a few warning shots toward the door before scrambling out after him. They landed in the narrow alley behind the motel, where the rain had turned the ground to mud.

"This way!" Langley motioned toward a side street.

They sprinted through the alley, the sound of boots pounding behind them. Mercer stole a glance over his shoulder. The gunmen were gaining.

"We need to split up," Langley panted. "They want me more than you. I'll lead them off—"

"Not a chance," Mercer cut him off. "We do this together."

Langley hesitated for half a second before nodding. "Then follow me and don't stop running."

They burst onto a main road, darting between parked cars. Gunfire cracked through the night, shattering a windshield inch from Mercer's head. He gritted his teeth and pushed forward.

An old service tunnel loomed ahead, partially hidden behind a chain-link fence. Langley motioned toward it. "There!"

They vaulted over the fence just as more bullets whizzed past them. The tunnel was dark and smelled of mildew, but it was shelter.

Langley caught his breath. "We lost them. For now."

Mercer leaned against the damp wall, adrenaline still racing through his veins. "That was too close."

Langley exhaled. "They're done playing games. Next time, they won't miss."

Mercer straightened; eyes cold. "Then we make sure there isn't a next time."

Langley met his gaze. "Agreed. But first, we need to find out who gave the kill order. Because they're not just coming for us. They're coming for everyone who ever stood against them."

Mercer clenched his fists. "Then let's start hunting."

XVII

The Enemy Within

The silence inside the service tunnel was suffocating. The only sound was the slow drip of water from somewhere in the darkness, echoing through the concrete walls like a metronome counting down to something inevitable. Mercer wiped the sweat from his brow and glanced at Langley, who was still catching his breath.

"We can't stay here long," Mercer muttered. "They'll be sweeping the area soon."

Langley nodded, still gripping his side where the impact of the chase had left a deep bruise. "We need a way to fight back. Running isn't going to cut it anymore."

Mercer's phone vibrated in his pocket. He pulled it out and saw an anonymous message flashing on the screen:

You're out of time, Detective. Ridgewood PD isn't safe anymore.

A chill ran down Mercer's spine. "They've infiltrated the station."

Langley frowned. "You sure?"

Mercer turned the screen to show him the message. "Someone on the inside is feeding them intel. That means

Wilkes, Claire, and anyone else I trust could be compromised."

Langley's expression hardened. "Then we need to find out who the rat is."

A Dangerous Gamble

Mercer and Langley made their way through the underground tunnels until they reached a drainage exit that led into the woods near the outskirts of town. They stayed low, avoiding the occasional squad car sweeping the streets with searchlights. The enemy was mobilizing, and they weren't taking any chances.

"We need a new base of operations," Langley muttered. "Somewhere off the grid."

Mercer thought for a moment, then snapped his fingers. "The old shipping yard by the docks. It's been abandoned for years. My uncle used to work security there—said nobody ever checked it."

Langley smirked. "Sounds like our kind of place. Let's move."

The Betrayal

An hour later, the shipping yard loomed in front of them, rusting metal containers stacked high against the misty night sky. The scent of salt and oil filled the air. Mercer and Langley entered cautiously, checking the area before slipping into one of the empty warehouses.

Langley set down his duffel bag and pulled out a laptop. "We need to figure out who's selling you out at the station. I had some old contacts dig into the department's recent financials—let's see if anything suspicious turns up."

As he typed, Mercer paced, mind racing. He hated the thought that someone inside his own department was working against him. His gut told him it wasn't Wilkes—he'd known the man too long. But Claire? Maybe. Another officer? Possible.

A beep from Langley's laptop made them both freeze.

"Got something," Langley said. "Anonymous deposits into an officer's account over the past six months. Large sums."

Mercer stepped closer. "Who?"

Langley's face darkened. "Officer Paul Simmons."

Mercer's blood boiled. "That son of a bitch."

Simmons had always been an unremarkable officer—quiet, efficient, never made waves. But that was the perfect cover. If he was working for the people hunting Mercer, then it made sense how they always seemed one step ahead.

Langley closed the laptop. "So, what's the plan? We walk into the station and put a gun to his head?"

Mercer shook his head. "No. We make him come to us."

Setting the Trap

Mercer sent Simmons a text from a burner phone: *I know who you work for. Meet me at Pier 22. Alone. One hour.*

He turned to Langley. "We make him think we have proof. He'll show up to eliminate the problem."

Langley smirked. "And we make sure he gets a surprise instead."

The Confrontation

The docks were deserted by the time Simmons arrived. Mercer watched from the shadows as the officer stepped out of his car, scanning the area nervously. His hand hovered near his gun.

Langley whispered, "He's expecting an ambush."

Mercer nodded. "Let's give him one."

They stepped out, guns raised. "Drop it, Simmons. It's over."

Simmons froze, then sighed. "Damn it, Mercer. Why couldn't you just let this go?"

"Because people are dying," Mercer shot back. "And you're helping make that happen. Who are you working for?"

Simmons clenched his jaw. "You don't get it. It's bigger than you. Bigger than all of us. They own everything. You can't win."

Mercer took a step closer. "Then why are you here? If they're so powerful, why not run back to them?"

Simmons swallowed hard. "Because they don't let people run. I'm already dead."

Langley tensed. "He's stalling."

Too late, Mercer saw Simmons' finger twitch. He reached for his gun—but before he could pull it, a shot rang out.

Simmons crumpled to the ground, a bullet hole between his eyes.

Mercer spun; gun raised. A shadow moved at the edge of the docks. A tall figure in a dark coat, barely visible in the mist.

Then, they were gone.

Langley cursed. "Who the hell was that?"

Mercer holstered his gun. "Someone cleaning up loose ends. And we're next."

Langley exhaled. "Then we better find them before they find us."

Mercer nodded. "And this time, we don't wait for them to make the first move."

XVIII

Closing the Noose

The night air was thick with mist as Mercer and Langley left the docks, the echoes of gunfire still ringing in their ears. The shadowy figure that had executed Simmons had disappeared without a trace, and now, they were running out of time.

Langley kept glancing over his shoulder as they walked toward their car. "You know that wasn't just a clean-up job. That was a warning."

Mercer nodded, gripping the steering wheel as he pulled away from the docks. "They know we're getting close. And now, they're making their moves."

Langley pulled out his laptop in the passenger seat, fingers flying across the keyboard. "We need to figure out who's calling the shots. Kane was powerful, but someone else is tying up the loose ends."

Mercer's phone buzzed. A blocked number. He hesitated, then answered. "Mercer."

A distorted voice filtered through the speaker. "Detective, you've gone too far. Walk away, or you won't get another chance."

Mercer's grip on the phone tightened. "Who the hell are you?"

The caller chuckled. "You already know. You just don't want to believe it."

The line went dead.

Langley stared at him. "Well, that was ominous."

Mercer tossed the phone onto the dashboard. "They're getting desperate. That means we're close."

The Safe House Breached

The old shipping yard had been their temporary refuge, but when Mercer and Langley arrived, the sight before them made their stomachs drop.

The warehouse door was wide open, swinging slightly in the wind. Inside, the space had been torn apart—papers shredded; the laptop Langley had left behind smashed beyond repair. Bullet holes riddled the metal walls.

"Damn it," Langley hissed. "They knew. They knew where we were."

Mercer scanned the destruction. "They're cleaning house. Erasing every trace of what we found."

Langley knelt, sifting through the wreckage. "Whoever did this was in a hurry. They weren't looking for us—they were making sure we wouldn't find something."

Mercer's eyes locked onto a single intact object in the chaos—a file folder, slightly singed but still readable. He picked it up and flipped through the pages. It was a list of financial transactions, offshore accounts, and, at the bottom, one name:

Senator Malcolm Vance.

Langley whistled. "Now that's a name worth killing for."

Mercer nodded grimly. "Looks like we just found the man pulling the strings."

A Dangerous Lead

Senator Vance was an untouchable figure in Ridgewood. A man whose power extended beyond the city, whose influence kept people like Kane in check. If he was behind the conspiracy, they weren't just up against corrupt cops anymore—they were taking on something much bigger.

Langley tapped at his new laptop, eyes scanning the screen. "Vance has deep ties to Ridgewood. He owns half the real estate downtown through shell companies. He's been funding projects through the police department for years. If Simmons was taking money, it probably came from him."

Mercer exhaled. "Then we need to get to Vance before he knows we're coming."

Langley gave him a look. "And how do you propose we do that? The man has more security than the damn governor."

Mercer smirked. "Then we don't go to him. We make him come to us."

The Setup

Mercer knew that Vance wouldn't respond to threats. He was too powerful, too careful. But there was one thing men like him feared—exposure.

They sent an anonymous tip to one of Ridgewood's top investigative journalists, feeding them just enough information to bait the hook. Within hours, Mercer's burner phone rang.

A deep, controlled voice came through. "Detective Mercer. I assume you're the one making waves."

Mercer didn't flinch. "Senator Vance. Funny, I thought you'd be harder to reach."

"And I thought you'd be smarter than to play a game you can't win," Vance replied smoothly. "I know what you think you've found, but let me assure you, you're out of your depth. Walk away, and this all goes away."

Mercer chuckled darkly. "That's not how this works. You see, I have evidence. And in about six hours, it's going public. Unless you meet me."

A pause.

Then Vance sighed. "Fine. Midnight. The old courthouse. Come alone."

Mercer hung up and looked at Langley. "Think he'll show?"

Langley grinned. "Oh, he'll show. But not alone."

Mercer nodded. "Then we go prepared."

The Courthouse Showdown

Midnight. The old courthouse stood empty, its grand structure now a ghost of Ridgewood's past. Mercer stood in the center of the main hall, heart steady, eyes scanning every shadow.

Footsteps.

Vance entered, flanked by two men in dark suits, their hands hovering near their concealed weapons.

"Detective Mercer," Vance greeted smoothly. "Quite the meeting place. Very dramatic."

Mercer crossed his arms. "I thought it suited the occasion."

Vance smirked. "Let's get to the point. You don't have anything. If you did, you wouldn't be standing here."

Mercer pulled out the file. "Oh, but I do. Offshore accounts. Shell companies. Bribes to police officers, including Simmons. You've been sloppy."

Vance's expression darkened. "And what do you plan to do with it?"

Mercer smiled. "Depends on what you say next."

A single gunshot rang out.

One of Vance's men collapsed, a bullet clean through his skull. The second barely had time to react before Langley emerged from the shadows, gun raised.

"Looks like the odds just changed," Langley said with a smirk.

Vance raised his hands, eyes cold. "You've made a mistake, Mercer. You don't know who you're really up against."

Mercer stepped forward. "Then why don't you enlighten me?"

XIX

The Tipping Point

Vance's smirk never wavered, even as his second bodyguard lay lifeless on the marble floor. Langley kept his gun steady, his finger hovering over the trigger. Mercer could feel the tension thickening in the air, the weight of an impending storm that neither side wanted to break first.

"This isn't going to end the way you think," Vance said smoothly, brushing non-existent dust off his tailored suit. "You don't kill a man like me and walk away."

Mercer took a slow step forward. "We don't need to kill you, Vance. We just need you to talk. And considering you're running out of people willing to die for you, I'd start answering some questions."

Vance sighed, rubbing his temple as if Mercer were nothing more than a mild inconvenience. "Detective Mercer, you really are persistent. That's admirable. Foolish, but admirable."

Langley cocked his gun. "Enough with the speeches. You either talk, or you get a bullet just like your men."

A slow clap echoed through the vast courthouse chamber. Mercer's gut twisted before he even turned to see who it was.

A tall man in a dark coat stepped from the shadows, his gloved hands now resting at his sides. Mercer recognized him instantly.

The Architect.

"Now, now," the man said, his voice like oil sliding over steel. "No need for rash decisions. Let's talk like civilized men."

The Mastermind Revealed

Langley stiffened, gun shifting toward the new arrival. "You son of a bitch."

Mercer's pulse pounded, but he forced himself to stay calm. "You finally decided to show your face."

The Architect smiled; his expression unreadable. "You've been making a mess, detective. Digging where you shouldn't. Killing people who were very useful to me. It's become... inconvenient."

Vance exhaled sharply. "What the hell is this? You told me—"

The Architect raised a hand, silencing him. "I told you what you needed to hear, Senator. That's what I do. I build narratives. I shape reality. And right now, reality is changing."

Mercer took a step forward. "You've been in the shadows long enough. Time to step into the light."

The Architect tilted his head. "And why would I do that, when the shadows have served me so well?"

Langley's grip on his gun tightened. "Because we have evidence. Names, accounts, transactions—enough to burn everything you built to the ground."

The Architect chuckled. "Oh, you sweet, naïve man. Evidence? You mean the files in that little warehouse? The ones I had destroyed hours ago?"

Mercer's stomach dropped.

Langley whispered, "No..."

The Architect nodded. "I know everything, gentlemen. Every move you've made, every call you've taken. Your allies? Most of them are dead or turning against you as we speak."

Vance's face drained of colour. "You set me up."

The Architect offered him a small, almost pitying smile. "You were never in control, Malcolm. You were just another piece on the board. And now, you're an obsolete one."

A single silenced gunshot rang out. Vance's head snapped back, blood misting the air before he crumpled to the floor.

Langley's gun fired a half-second later, but The Architect was already moving, vanishing into the darkness.

"Mercer, move!" Langley shouted, yanking him back as more gunmen stormed into the courthouse, their rifles barking fire.

The Escape

The next few moments were a blur of bullets and movement. Mercer ducked behind an overturned bench, returning fire as Langley covered him. The Architect's men were well-trained, methodical—mercenaries, not street thugs.

"We're boxed in!" Langley called over the chaos.

Mercer's mind worked fast. "Back exit!"

They sprinted for the hallway, bullets tearing into the wooden paneling as they ran. Langley kicked open a side door, and they burst into the night air, skidding onto the courthouse steps.

A black SUV screeched onto the curb, its doors flying open.

Wilkes.

"Get in!" he bellowed.

Mercer and Langley dove into the vehicle as Wilkes hit the gas, tires screeching. Gunfire followed them down the street, shattering the rear windshield.

"Jesus Christ," Wilkes gritted his teeth, swerving onto an empty highway. "What the hell did you two just do?"

Langley exhaled sharply. "We just declared war."

Mercer clenched his jaw, staring at the fading city lights in the rearview mirror. "And we're not losing."

The Aftermath

They regrouped at an old auto shop Wilkes owned outside of town. The place smelled like oil and dust, but it was safe.

Wilkes paced. "You tell me right now—are we screwed?"

Langley leaned against a workbench. "Not yet. But we're close."

Mercer exhaled. "Vance is dead. The Architect is real, and now we have a target on our backs."

Wilkes rubbed his face. "Fantastic."

Langley pulled out his phone. "We still have options. But we have to move fast."

Mercer met his gaze. "Then let's finish this. Once and for all."

XX

Into the Fire

The garage was silent except for the hum of a single overhead light, casting flickering shadows against the oil-stained concrete. Mercer leaned against the workbench, studying the map Langley had laid out. A red circle marked their next target—a high-rise penthouse in the city's financial district.

"That's where The Architect is holed up," Langley muttered. "I hacked into his security feeds. The place is a fortress—private elevators, biometric locks, armed guards at every entrance. We go in loud; we don't make it out."

Wilkes leaned against the wall, arms crossed. "So, what's the alternative? We walk up to the front desk and ask nicely?"

Mercer's gaze darkened. "No. We find another way in."

Langley tapped the map. "There's a maintenance shaft that runs through the building. If we can access it, we can bypass security and reach the penthouse."

Wilkes exhaled. "Jesus. You two are really gonna do this."

Mercer met his gaze. "We don't have a choice. The Architect won't stop until we're dead. This is our one shot."

Wilkes sighed. "Then let's make it count."

Breaking In

The high-rise loomed above them, its glass windows reflecting the city lights. Mercer adjusted his earpiece as Langley worked on the maintenance panel behind the building. The seconds stretched as he bypassed the system.

"And... we're in," Langley whispered. The door clicked open.

They slipped inside, navigating through the dimly lit corridors until they reached the service elevator. Langley pulled out a tablet, hacking into the system. "I can override the lockdown, but we'll have a small window to reach the top."

Mercer checked his gun. "Then let's move fast."

The elevator doors slid open, and they stepped inside. The ride up was silent, tension coiled in their muscles. The doors opened to a lavish penthouse, floor-to-ceiling windows revealing the city skyline. And standing by the glass, waiting, was The Architect.

The Final Confrontation

The Architect turned, a knowing smile on his face. "I was beginning to think you wouldn't show."

Mercer raised his gun. "It's over."

The Architect chuckled. "Over? No, detective. It's just beginning."

The room erupted in chaos as hidden guards emerged, weapons drawn. Gunfire roared through the penthouse. Mercer dove for cover as Langley returned fire. Wilkes took down two guards, but more poured in from the side rooms.

"We're outnumbered!" Langley yelled.

Mercer's mind raced. Then he saw it—The Architect moving toward a hidden passage behind his desk.

"He's running!" Mercer broke cover, charging forward.

The Architect slipped through the passage. Mercer followed, emerging onto the rooftop. The wind howled as The Architect stood at the edge, looking down at the streets below.

"You don't understand, Mercer," The Architect said, his voice almost calm. "Even if you kill me, this doesn't end. There's always someone waiting to take my place."

Mercer's grip on his gun tightened. "Then I'll make sure you don't get that chance."

The Architect smirked. "You think you're the hero of this story? You're just another piece in the game."

Mercer pulled the trigger.

A single gunshot echoed into the night.

XXI

The Fall of the Architect

The gunshot rang out, piercing through the night like a crack of thunder. Mercer kept his gun raised, the weight of the moment pressing against his ribs. The Architect staggered backward, his smirk faltering as a dark stain spread across his chest. He swayed at the edge of the rooftop, the wind howling around him.

Langley burst onto the roof; gun drawn. "Mercer!"

The Architect coughed, blood staining his lips, but he didn't fall. Instead, he chuckled—a hoarse, chilling sound. "You think this ends with me?"

Mercer took a slow step forward, his finger still on the trigger. "You're done. Your operation is finished."

The Architect grinned despite the blood dripping down his chin. "You naive fool. The real power? It doesn't die with a bullet. It just finds a new host."

Mercer's stomach twisted. "Who are you working for?"

The Architect exhaled sharply, his knees buckling. "Wouldn't you like to know..."

With a final, deliberate step, he let himself fall backward.

Mercer lunged, but it was too late. The Architect disappeared into the fog below, his body swallowed by the darkness.

Langley ran to the edge, peering down. "Did you see—?"

Mercer's jaw tightened. "No body."

Wilkes' voice crackled over the radio. "Mercer, we need you downstairs. Now."

The Cleanup

The penthouse was in shambles. Bullet casings littered the floor, and the lingering scent of gunpowder mixed with expensive cologne. Several of The Architect's men lay dead, but a few had been taken into custody.

Wilkes met Mercer at the doorway, his expression unreadable. "We got some of them, but the head of the snake is gone."

Mercer holstered his gun. "He's not dead. Not until we see a body."

Langley sighed. "So what now? We comb through every alley, every exit point? He planned this. He had an escape route."

Mercer turned to one of the captured men, a tall, wiry enforcer with a busted lip. "Where would he go?"

The man sneered. "You have no idea what you're up against, do you?"

Mercer grabbed him by the collar. "Enlighten me."

The enforcer smirked. "You think he's the only one? There are others. You may have burned down one house, but the whole city is built on rot."

Wilkes pulled Mercer back before he did something regrettable. "We'll get what we can out of them, but he's right. This goes deeper."

Langley exhaled. "We need to vanish. If The Architect survived, he won't stop until we're dead."

Mercer nodded. "Then we vanish. But we don't stop. We find every last one of them. And this time, we don't just break their empire. We burn it to the ground."

Wilkes gave a tight nod. "Then let's get to work."

Epilogue: The Shadows Remain

Weeks passed, but Ridgewood didn't change. The news barely mentioned the penthouse shootout, brushing it off as a 'gang-related incident.' The names of the dead were forgotten. And The Architect? No sightings. No body.

Mercer stood by his car, watching the city lights flicker in the distance. Langley leaned against the hood, arms crossed.

"You still think he's out there?" Langley asked.

Mercer's eyes narrowed. "I don't think. I know."

Wilkes stepped up, handing Mercer a folder. "We got a new lead. An offshore account just got accessed. Big money. And guess who had ties to it?"

Mercer opened the folder. Inside was a blurry security photo of a man boarding a private jet.

The Architect.

Mercer closed the folder. "Looks like the hunt isn't over."

Langley smirked. "Then let's go hunting."

The night stretched before them, full of unanswered questions. But one thing was certain.

The shadows had not yet lifted.

And Mercer wasn't done.

XXII

The Ghost That Wouldn't Die

The air in Ridgewood had changed. Mercer could feel it in his bones. The Architect was gone—at least that's what the world believed. But Mercer knew better. No body. No closure. And now, a new storm was brewing.

Langley stood beside him in the dimly lit parking garage, eyes fixed on his laptop screen. "I ran another search. Offshore accounts we traced to Vance? Someone's still moving the money."

Mercer's stomach tightened. "It's him."

Wilkes, leaning against the hood of their car, shook his head. "Or someone picking up where he left off. Either way, this isn't over."

A phone rang. Not Mercer's. Not Langley's. A burner phone, left in the glove compartment. The one only a handful of people knew about.

Mercer picked it up. "Who is this?"

A familiar, chilling voice rasped through the speaker. "Miss me, detective?"

Mercer's blood ran cold. The Architect was alive.

Langley and Wilkes watched as Mercer's grip on the phone tightened.

"You should've made sure I was dead, Mercer," the voice continued. "Now, it's my turn."

The call cut off.

Langley's eyes darted to Mercer. "We need to move. Now."

Mercer exhaled slowly, forcing himself to think. "No. We don't run. We hunt."

Wilkes cracked his knuckles. "Then let's finish this."

XXIII

A Game of Shadows

The night air was thick with tension as Mercer, Langley, and Wilkes sat in the dim glow of a rundown diner just outside Ridgewood. The Architect's call had changed everything. They had thought they were close to the end, but now, it was clear—they had only been chasing ghosts.

Langley tapped away at his laptop, the faint blue light illuminating his focused expression. "I rerouted the signal from the burner phone. The call didn't originate from Ridgewood—it was bounced through multiple locations. But the last traceable ping? Southside docks."

Wilkes groaned. "Figures. That place is a death trap. Gangs, traffickers, and now, The Architect's goons? This just keeps getting better."

Mercer took a sip of his coffee, his mind running through possibilities. "He's playing us. He wants us to come to him. But why now? He could've stayed hidden. Why make contact?"

Langley glanced up. "Because he's setting a trap. And he wants you in it."

Wilkes exhaled. "So we spring it. On our terms."

Mercer nodded. "We go in quiet, recon only. If he's there, we take him. If not, we find out what he's planning."

Langley smirked. "I'll get the gear."

Wilkes cracked his knuckles. "Then let's go hunting."

The Setup

The Southside docks were a forgotten part of Ridgewood, a place where deals were made in the shadows and bodies disappeared without a trace. The trio parked a block away, moving in on foot.

Langley set up a surveillance drone, feeding live footage to his tablet. "Two guards at the main gate. Another three patrolling. Heavy firepower. They're expecting company."

Wilkes scanned the area. "No sign of The Architect."

Mercer's eyes narrowed. "That doesn't mean he's not watching."

They moved in, sticking to the shadows. As they approached a rusted shipping container marked with an old corporate logo, Langley's voice crackled through the earpiece.

"Mercer, hold up. You're gonna want to see this."

Mercer crouched behind a stack of wooden pallets as Langley sent him a live video feed. Inside the container, strapped to a chair, was a man Mercer recognized immediately.

Chief Donovan.

His former boss. The one man who had protected Mercer when this case had first spiraled out of control.

Wilkes swore under his breath. "That's one hell of a message."

Mercer's grip on his gun tightened. "We're going in. Now."

The Ambush

The moment they stepped into the open, the trap was sprung. Gunfire erupted from the rooftops, bullets slamming into the ground around them.

"Cover!" Mercer shouted, diving behind a stack of barrels as Wilkes returned fire. Langley scrambled behind a crate, frantically typing on his tablet.

"They jammed our signal! No drone, no backup!" Langley yelled.

Mercer cursed. "We need to get to Donovan before they move him!"

Wilkes fired off a shot, hitting one of the snipers. "Then let's move!"

They charged forward, bullets flying past them as they reached the container. Mercer kicked open the door, gun raised.

Inside, Donovan looked up, bloodied but conscious. "Mercer... it's a trap..."

Before Mercer could respond, the speakers inside the container crackled to life.

"You walked right into this one, Detective," The Architect's voice sneered. "And now, it's checkmate."

A metallic beep echoed.

Wilkes' eyes widened. "Mercer, bomb!"

The world exploded in fire and smoke.

XXIV

Smoke and Ashes

The explosion ripped through the container, sending shockwaves through the docks. Mercer felt himself being thrown backward, the heat searing his skin as he crashed against the concrete. His ears rang, the world around him a blur of fire, smoke, and screams.

"Mercer!" Langley's voice cut through the chaos.

Mercer groaned, pushing himself up. His vision swam, but he forced himself to focus. The container was in flames, metal twisted and burning. Wilkes was already on his feet, scanning the area, gun raised. "We need to move!"

Mercer coughed, waving away the smoke. "Donovan—where's Donovan?"

Langley was already moving toward the wreckage, but the fire was too intense. "I—I don't see him!"

A crackling sound came from the speakers, distorted by static. The Architect's voice, calm as ever, rang through the docks.

"I told you, Detective. This was always my game. And you? You're just another piece on the board."

Wilkes fired a shot at the nearest speaker, but the voice continued, playing from multiple sources around them.

"You think you're close to stopping me? You have no idea what's coming. Ridgewood isn't yours to save, Mercer. It belongs to the shadows."

Mercer's jaw clenched as he scanned the area. They were sitting ducks. They needed to get out—now.

The Escape

Gunfire erupted again, forcing them to duck behind a row of shipping crates. Shadows moved through the smoke, figures with automatic rifles closing in.

"We're outnumbered!" Langley yelled, reloading.

Mercer grabbed Wilkes' radio. "We need an extraction. Now."

Wilkes fired off another round. "Who the hell do you think is coming? We're on our own!"

Mercer's mind raced. Then he saw it—an old maintenance truck near the edge of the docks. If they could reach it, they could get out.

"Cover me!" Mercer shouted, sprinting toward the truck. Bullets kicked up the ground around him, but he kept moving. He reached the door, wrenched it open, and hot-wired the ignition. The engine roared to life.

"Move! Now!"

Langley and Wilkes made a break for it, diving into the truck as Mercer floored the gas. The vehicle barreled through crates and debris, the gunmen disappearing into the smoke behind them.

As they sped down the highway, silence filled the cab, broken only by the distant sound of sirens. Langley wiped blood from his forehead, exhaling sharply.

"We lost him again."

Mercer gripped the wheel, knuckles white. "No. This isn't over."

Wilkes sighed. "Then where do we go from here?"

Mercer stared ahead, his mind already working. "We find the next breadcrumb. And this time, we don't stop until The Architect is buried for good."

XXV

A Trail of Blood

The battered maintenance truck screeched to a halt in a desolate warehouse district on the outskirts of Ridgewood. Mercer killed the engine, gripping the wheel tightly. The weight of failure sat heavy on his chest. The Architect had slipped through their fingers—again.

Langley wiped at the blood on his forehead, wincing. "We need a plan, and we need it now."

Wilkes exhaled sharply, checking the magazine on his pistol. "That wasn't just an ambush. That was a damn statement. He wanted us to walk into that fire, knowing we wouldn't get out clean."

Mercer leaned back against the seat, eyes scanning the darkened streets outside. "He's pushing us. Testing how far we'll go."

Langley looked up from his laptop, his fingers flying across the keys. "I might have something. There's a bank transaction—heavy movement of funds, routed through dummy corporations. The last pinged location? A private airstrip an hour from here. Someone's trying to leave Ridgewood."

Wilkes cracked his knuckles. "Then we make sure they don't."

The Airstrip

The night was thick with humidity as they approached the private airstrip, hidden behind rows of industrial buildings and chain-link fences. A sleek black jet sat on the tarmac, its engines humming softly.

Mercer pulled the truck into the shadows, cutting the lights. "This is it. If The Architect's here, this might be our only shot."

Langley adjusted his earpiece. "Thermal scans show six hostiles near the plane. Two by the hangar, another two patrolling. The last two? Likely on board already."

Wilkes chambered a round. "So, what's the play?"

Mercer's expression was stone-cold. "We move in quiet, take them before they know what's happening. If The Architect's inside, we end this. Tonight."

Langley swallowed. "No backup, no second chances."

"Just the way we like it," Mercer muttered.

The Assault

The first guard never saw Mercer coming. A swift, brutal strike to the throat sent him crumpling without a sound. Wilkes dropped the second with a silenced shot.

They moved fast, slipping past the security checkpoint and toward the plane. A pair of men near the boarding ramp were speaking in hushed tones. Mercer could hear the urgency in their voices.

"We need to move—now. He's expecting us."

Mercer exchanged a look with Wilkes. *He.* Someone was waiting for The Architect. And whoever it was, they were powerful enough to make him run.

Wilkes raised his pistol, ready to take the shot—

But then the unexpected happened.

From inside the plane, a familiar voice echoed through the night. A voice Mercer hadn't heard in years.

"Stand down, Mercer. This isn't your fight anymore."

Mercer's breath hitched. His gun hand wavered.

Wilkes frowned. "Mercer? Who the hell is that?"

Mercer's grip tightened. "My past."

Langley's voice crackled through the earpiece. "We got a problem. Big one. The Architect isn't alone. There's someone else inside. Someone with high-level clearance. This whole thing just got a lot worse."

Mercer's mind raced. If the voice he heard was real, it meant everything he thought he knew about this case was a lie.

And if that was true...

Then The Architect wasn't the one pulling the strings after all.

XXVI

The Betrayal

A tense silence fell over the airstrip as Mercer's gun remained fixed on the open door of the jet. The voice had struck him like a hammer to the chest—unmistakable, haunting. A voice from the past.

Wilkes shifted beside him. "Mercer, you gonna tell me what the hell is going on?"

Mercer's grip tightened. "That voice... it belongs to someone who should be dead."

Before Wilkes or Langley could press for more, a figure emerged from the shadows inside the jet. Dressed in a black tactical vest, with streaks of gray in his once-dark hair, was **Elias Kane.**

Mercer's breath hitched. Kane—his former mentor, his closest ally—had died years ago. Or so he thought.

Kane stepped forward, his hands raised slightly, a smirk playing at his lips. "It's been a long time, kid. Didn't think you'd make it this far."

Langley's voice crackled in Mercer's earpiece. "Mercer... that's not possible. Kane was declared dead in a car bombing six years ago. The case was closed."

Mercer swallowed the rising storm of emotions. "Looks like they got that wrong."

Wilkes raised his gun. "What the hell is this?"

Kane's smirk deepened. "It's the part where you realize everything you thought you knew about this case is a lie."

The Truth Unveiled

Mercer stepped closer, his voice sharp. "You worked with me, trained me. And then you died. So tell me, Kane, how the hell are you standing in front of me?"

Kane sighed, rolling his shoulders. "I didn't die. I disappeared. And I had to, Mercer. Because I saw what was coming. The Architect? He's just a symptom. The real disease runs deeper."

Wilkes scoffed. "That's cute. You expect us to believe you're some martyr? You let people think you were dead. You let Mercer bury you."

Kane's eyes darkened. "Because I had no choice. The people I was working against, they don't just kill you. They erase you. I had to vanish before they made that decision for me."

Mercer took a slow breath, trying to steady the fury rising in his chest. "And now you're back? Why? Why now?"

Kane glanced at the jet. "Because it's time to finish what I started. And whether you like it or not, you're a part of it."

Langley's voice came through the comms. "Mercer, we've got movement—four SUVs inbound. Fast."

Kane turned toward the sound of approaching engines. "Looks like my time's up."

The Escape

Gunfire erupted as the SUVs skidded to a stop, doors flying open. Armed men in tactical gear poured out, weapons raised. Mercer barely had time to react before bullets tore through the air.

"Go!" Kane yelled, diving back into the jet.

Mercer cursed but followed, Wilkes and Langley close behind. The moment they were inside, Kane slammed his fist against the cockpit wall. "Get us in the air! Now!"

The plane lurched forward, bullets ricocheting off the fuselage as the engines roared to life. Mercer braced himself as the jet accelerated, the wheels barely leaving the ground before the first explosion rocked the tarmac.

Langley cursed. "They had RPGs?!"

Wilkes gritted his teeth. "Yeah, because this wasn't an ambush. This was an execution."

Mercer turned to Kane, his voice razor-sharp. "Start talking. Now."

Kane exhaled. "Buckle up, kid. Because you just crossed a line you can't come back from."

Mercer's jaw clenched. "Then let's finish what we started."

XXVII

A Flight into Darkness

The hum of the jet's engines filled the cabin, but the tension between Mercer and Kane was louder. Langley kept checking the radar on his laptop, eyes darting between screens. Wilkes sat across from Kane, pistol resting on his knee, ready for the slightest reason to pull the trigger.

Mercer folded his arms. "Talk. Now."

Kane sighed, running a hand through his graying hair. "You're not ready for the truth, kid."

Mercer's jaw clenched. "Try me."

Kane leaned forward. "The Architect was never the real threat. He was a piece—an important one—but nothing more than a puppet. The real power? It's still out there, and it knows we're coming."

Langley cut in. "And who, exactly, are we dealing with?"

Kane exhaled. "A group known as **The Dominion**. They've had their hands in Ridgewood's corruption for decades. Government, corporations, law enforcement—it's all connected. They don't just control the city. They own it."

Wilkes shook his head. "So what? You faked your death to go after them? And now you expect us to help?"

Kane's expression hardened. "I don't expect anything. But if we don't take them down, they'll bury us before we get another shot. The Architect was their enforcer. Now that he's gone, they'll send someone worse."

Mercer's eyes narrowed. "And you know this how?"

Kane hesitated, then pulled a tablet from his bag. He tapped the screen, flipping it toward Mercer. A grainy security photo appeared—taken from a high-rise balcony. A man stood with his back to the camera, but his posture, the way he carried himself, felt eerily familiar.

Langley squinted at the image. "Who is that?"

Kane's voice was grim. "The one they call **Silas**. He's their fixer. The man who eliminates problems. And right now? We're the biggest problem they have."

The Intercept

Before Mercer could process Kane's words, Langley's laptop beeped sharply. His fingers flew across the keyboard. "Uh, we've got company. Fast movers on radar. Two unknown aircraft inbound."

Wilkes cursed. "They found us."

Kane didn't even look surprised. "Told you."

The cockpit door slid open, the pilot shouting back, "We've got incoming! Missiles locked!"

Mercer grabbed a headset. "Evasive maneuvers!"

The jet banked hard, sending everyone crashing against the cabin walls. Langley clung to his laptop, trying to override the targeting systems. "I might be able to jam their lock, but I need time!"

Wilkes braced himself. "We don't have time!"

Kane moved toward a weapons locker, flipping it open. Inside were high-caliber rifles, emergency parachutes, and a single shoulder-mounted missile launcher. He tossed a rifle to Wilkes. "You still know how to shoot?"

Wilkes grinned. "Like riding a bike."

Mercer grabbed the launcher. "How many shots?"

"One," Kane said. "So make it count."

Mercer moved to the hatch, gripping a safety strap as he forced the door open. The wind howled, nearly tearing him off his feet. The pursuing aircraft loomed closer, their weapons systems blinking red.

Langley's voice crackled through the earpiece. "You need to take the shot now!"

Mercer aimed. His breath slowed. His pulse steadied. Then he fired.

The missile spiraled through the night sky, striking the lead jet dead center. A fireball erupted, sending the second aircraft veering off course.

Wilkes whooped. "Hell yeah!"

But before they could celebrate, Kane's voice cut through the moment.

"Strap in. We're going down."

Mercer turned. "What?!"

Kane pointed to the cockpit. Smoke filled the control panels. "We took a hit. We're not making it to the destination. Brace for impact!"

The jet spiraled, alarms blaring. The last thing Mercer saw was the ground rushing toward them before everything went black.

XXVIII
Wreckage and Ruin

Pain. That was the first thing Mercer registered. A deep, throbbing pain in his ribs and a sharp ringing in his ears. His vision swam as he blinked through smoke and darkness. The wreckage of the jet lay scattered across the forest floor, metal twisted and burning.

"Mercer!" A voice cut through the haze.

He turned his head, groaning. Langley was crouched beside him, blood trickling down his temple. "You good? Can you move?"

Mercer forced himself upright, his body protesting with every movement. He glanced around. Wilkes was already on his feet, helping Kane out of the wreckage.

"Everyone alive?" Mercer coughed, wiping soot from his face.

"Barely," Wilkes muttered. "We need to move. Now."

Kane, still catching his breath, gestured toward the trees. "We weren't the only ones tracking this flight. If Silas is half as good as I remember, his men are already inbound."

Langley checked his laptop, grimacing. "Satellite uplink's fried. We're blind. No comms, no backup."

Mercer exhaled sharply. "Then we do what we do best. We disappear."

The Hunt Begins

The dense forest provided cover, but it also made it easier for their pursuers to set an ambush. Mercer led the team through the underbrush, his senses razor-sharp. Every snapped twig, every distant rustle of leaves could be an enemy closing in.

Langley whispered, "I count at least six heat signatures moving toward the wreckage. They're sweeping the area."

Wilkes readied his rifle. "What's the play?"

Kane crouched behind a fallen tree, scanning the approaching figures. "We let them think we died in the crash. Circle around, take them out quietly."

Mercer nodded. "We split up. Langley, find high ground. Wilkes, cover the flank. Kane, you're with me. We take them before they take us."

They moved in silence. The first enemy soldier passed beneath Langley's position, completely unaware. One well-placed shot with a silenced pistol, and he dropped like a stone.

Wilkes struck next, taking out a second with a knife to the throat before dragging the body into the shadows.

Mercer and Kane stalked the remaining four. One man knelt beside the wreckage, scanning for survivors. He never saw Mercer coming. A swift strike to the neck, and he was down.

Kane locked eyes with the last operative—a towering man with a scar running down his cheek. The man hesitated for only a second before raising his weapon.

Too late.

Kane put a bullet between his eyes.

Silence fell over the forest. The only sounds were the crackling of the wreckage and their own ragged breaths.

Langley rejoined them, wiping his hands on his pants. "That's six down. How many more do you think Silas sent?"

Kane didn't answer immediately. Instead, he knelt beside one of the fallen soldiers, pulling a small device from his vest. A blinking red light.

Mercer's stomach sank. "Tracker."

Kane nodded grimly. "Which means Silas knows exactly where we are. And he's sending more."

Wilkes wiped blood from his knife. "Then we need to stop running. We make our stand."

Mercer took a slow breath, his mind racing. "Then we set a trap. We turn the hunters into the hunted."

Kane smirked. "Now you're thinking like a survivor."

Langley cracked his knuckles. "Good. Because I think we just ran out of places to hide."

XXIX

The Silent Hour

The forest was unnervingly quiet. Too quiet. Mercer had learned long ago that silence in the middle of a hunt wasn't peace—it was the sound of a predator waiting to strike.

Langley crouched low behind a thick tree, eyes flicking between his thermal scanner and the dark expanse of trees ahead. "They're here," he whispered. "Fifteen—no, sixteen hostiles. Moving in pairs."

Wilkes clenched his jaw. "We can't fight them head-on. We'll be shredded."

Mercer's mind raced. "We won't fight them head-on. We lead them into their own noose."

Kane smirked. "I like the way you think."

The Trap is Set

Moving with precision, the team planted makeshift traps—tripwires, pressure mines from the wreckage, and flares rigged to disorient. Mercer and Kane climbed into the thick branches of a nearby tree, rifles trained on the approaching figures.

Langley set up a remote signal jammer, ensuring The Dominion couldn't call in reinforcements. "They'll be blind once they enter this zone," he murmured.

"Then we make sure they never leave it," Mercer said coldly.

Minutes stretched into a tense eternity. Then, the first figure appeared—a soldier moving cautiously, rifle raised. Another followed. Then another.

Wilkes threw a rock into the undergrowth. The sound snapped their attention to the right, drawing them straight into the kill zone.

The first explosion ripped through the forest. Flames illuminated the trees as shouts of confusion erupted. The team struck fast. Mercer's rifle barked as one soldier dropped. Kane picked off another before they could react.

Chaos.

Bullets tore through the darkness. Explosions sent bodies flying. Langley's makeshift EMP fried their comms, leaving them isolated and panicked.

Silas' men tried to retreat—right into another set of traps. Wilkes emerged from the shadows, taking down two before they even knew he was there.

And then, just as suddenly as it had begun, the silence returned.

Smoke curled into the sky. The bodies of The Dominion's soldiers lay scattered.

Mercer lowered his rifle. "We're not done. Silas isn't here."

Kane, wiping blood from his knife, nodded. "Then we find him."

A Message from the Shadows

Langley's laptop beeped. He frowned, glancing at the screen. "We just got a message. Encrypted. Sent directly to us."

Wilkes stiffened. "Who the hell knows we're here?"

Mercer took the laptop. The message contained only three words:

You can't win.

And below it, a live feed flickered to life. A dimly lit warehouse. A man bound to a chair. Bloodied. Beaten.

Chief Donovan.

Kane's expression darkened. "Silas has him."

Mercer's hands curled into fists. "Then we finish this."

XXX

No Way Out

The dim light of Langley's laptop cast eerie shadows on their faces as they stared at the live feed. Chief Donovan, bloodied and bound, barely held his head up. The timestamp on the footage showed it was live.

"We move now," Mercer said, voice tight with fury.

Wilkes was already checking his rifle. "Where is this place?"

Langley's fingers flew over the keyboard. "The signal is bouncing off multiple relays, but I've got a lock. It's a warehouse just outside the city. Abandoned steel factory. Perfect place for an execution."

Kane exhaled slowly. "Silas isn't just holding Donovan for leverage. He's making a statement. If we walk in blind, we die."

Mercer holstered his gun. "Then we don't walk in blind. We bring hell to his doorstep."

Into the Wolf's Den

The warehouse loomed ahead, its skeletal frame outlined against the midnight sky. The air was thick with the scent of oil and rust. The perfect place for a slaughter.

Langley's voice crackled in Mercer's earpiece. "Two snipers on the roof. Six guards at the entrance. Another four patrolling the perimeter. And I guarantee there are more inside."

Wilkes adjusted his sights. "I can take the snipers."

Mercer gave a nod. "Do it. Langley, kill the power when we move in. Kane and I will breach from the back."

Wilkes exhaled slowly. The first shot rang out—a silenced whisper. The first sniper crumpled. A heartbeat later, the second went down.

"Clear," Wilkes whispered.

Langley hit the power grid. The warehouse plunged into darkness.

"Go!" Mercer hissed.

They moved quickly, weaving through the shadows. Kane took out a guard with a swift knife strike. Mercer silenced another with a suppressed shot.

The air inside was thick with tension. The distant hum of machinery masked their footsteps as they slipped deeper into the belly of the beast.

The Trap Springs

They reached the main hall. A single chair sat in the center, a dim light casting a pale glow over Chief Donovan.

Mercer motioned for Kane to cover him as he moved in. "Donovan?"

The Chief groaned, barely conscious. Blood dripped from his temple. But something was wrong.

Too easy.

Mercer's instincts screamed at him. He turned—

Too late.

A gunshot rang out. A searing pain exploded in Mercer's shoulder as he was thrown backward.

The shadows came alive. Dozens of armed men emerged from the darkness, rifles trained on them.

Silas stepped forward, slow and deliberate. He was tall, lean, his presence exuding quiet menace. He clapped his hands mockingly. "Detective Mercer. Always running toward the fire."

Kane tensed. "You should've stayed in the dark, Silas."

Silas smirked. "And you should've stayed dead."

The Double Cross

Mercer gritted his teeth, pressing a hand to his bleeding shoulder. "What do you want, Silas?"

Silas circled him like a predator playing with its prey. "You don't get it, do you? This isn't about winning or losing. The Dominion isn't an organization. It's an idea. And you? You're just a loose end."

Wilkes' voice crackled over the comm. "Mercer, we've got movement outside—more incoming. We're outnumbered."

Silas grinned. "Looks like your time's up."

Then, out of nowhere, a new voice echoed from the darkness.

"Actually, I think it's yours."

Gunfire erupted from above. The skylights shattered as armed figures repelled in, opening fire. The Dominion's men were caught off guard, chaos erupting as Mercer's unexpected backup stormed the warehouse.

Kane grinned. "You didn't think we came alone, did you?"

Silas' face twisted in rage. "Kill them all!"

The Final Stand

The battle exploded. Mercer ducked behind cover, firing with his good arm. Wilkes took out two guards, while Kane fought hand-to-hand, knife flashing.

Silas made a break for the exit.

"He's running!" Mercer shouted, pushing through the pain as he gave chase.

Silas burst into the open yard, heading for an armored SUV. Mercer forced his legs to move, adrenaline dulling the pain.

Silas turned, raising his gun—

Mercer fired first.

Silas staggered, clutching his chest. He dropped to his knees, eyes wide with shock.

Mercer stood over him, gun still trained. "Game over."

Silas coughed, blood staining his lips. He chuckled weakly. "You still don't get it, do you? The Dominion doesn't die with me. You'll never stop it."

Mercer's jaw tightened. "Maybe not. But I just stopped you."

Silas exhaled one last breath, then collapsed.

XXXI

Ashes and Echoes

The smoke from Silas' final breath had barely settled before Mercer felt the weight of the moment press down on him. The man who had been pulling the strings, orchestrating chaos, was finally dead. But as Silas had warned, The Dominion wouldn't die with him. If anything, it had just become more dangerous.

Langley's voice crackled in Mercer's earpiece. "We need to go. Now. I'm picking up encrypted chatter. Someone else is moving in."

Kane holstered his weapon, scanning the area. "Silas wasn't lying. He was just another piece on the board. The real players are still out there."

Wilkes wiped blood from his brow. "Then we get the hell out before they arrive. We regroup, figure out our next move."

Mercer glanced down at Silas' lifeless body. His words lingered. *You'll never stop it.*

Mercer clenched his jaw. "Then we burn their entire operation down."

The Pursuit

The team barely made it out of the warehouse before headlights flooded the compound. Black SUVs skidded onto the scene, armed men pouring out.

"Move!" Kane barked, leading them into the darkness.

Bullets tore through the night as they sprinted toward the emergency escape route Langley had mapped out. Mercer felt the sting of his wounded shoulder, but adrenaline kept him moving.

Wilkes spun mid-run, laying down suppressing fire. "Keep running! I'll slow them down."

Mercer grabbed his arm. "We leave together."

A bullet clipped Wilkes' side, sending him sprawling. Mercer and Kane hauled him up as Langley slammed open the emergency exit—an old sewer maintenance tunnel leading out to the docks.

"Inside! Now!" Langley shouted.

They disappeared into the tunnel just as more gunfire rained down behind them.

A Revelation in the Dark

They didn't stop running until they reached a safe house—an old, abandoned bar near the harbor. Langley sealed the entrance, double-checking the security feeds.

Kane set Wilkes down, inspecting his wound. "You'll live. Barely."

Wilkes winced. "Guess I'll have to cancel my vacation."

Mercer wiped blood from his face, his thoughts racing. "Silas was just a gatekeeper. We need to find out who he was protecting."

Langley pulled up data on his laptop. "I cloned Silas' phone before we left. There's a name. A single contact marked with priority clearance."

Mercer leaned in. "Who?"

Langley hesitated. "Director Henry Voss. Head of Ridgewood's intelligence division. If anyone knows The Dominion's full reach, it's him."

Kane exhaled. "Then we go after him."

Wilkes smirked. "Yeah? And how do we do that? Walk up to the most powerful man in the city and ask nicely?"

Mercer's expression darkened. "No. We make him come to us."

The Setup

Hours later, an encrypted email hit Director Voss' inbox.

We have the files. Proof of Dominion's operations. Meet us alone, or it all goes public.

A single reply came moments later.

Midnight. The old courthouse.

Mercer looked at the message and smiled grimly. "He took the bait."

Langley frowned. "This could be a trap."

Mercer nodded. "Probably is. But he doesn't know we expect it."

The Final Gambit

Midnight. The courthouse stood like a monolith of forgotten justice. Mercer, Kane, Langley, and Wilkes took positions. Voss arrived in a sleek black car, stepping out alone—his posture controlled, his presence exuding quiet authority.

"Detective Mercer," Voss said, his voice smooth. "You've been busy."

Mercer didn't lower his gun. "And you've been hiding. Silas is dead. You're next."

Voss smirked. "That's where you're wrong. Silas was necessary. A tool. But he was expendable. The Dominion is bigger than one man. It always has been."

Mercer's finger tightened on the trigger. "Then tell me—who's really running the show?"

Voss chuckled. "You're not ready for that truth. But don't worry. It's coming."

Before Mercer could react, Voss pressed something in his pocket. A detonation echoed in the distance.

Langley's laptop beeped frantically. "Oh, hell. That was a data wipe—he just erased everything."

Voss smiled. "You're playing a game you can't win. See you soon, detective."

Then, without another word, Voss turned and walked away, leaving Mercer standing in the ruins of another dead lead.

XXXII

The Gathering Storm

Mercer stood in the dimly lit safe house, staring at the city skyline through a cracked window. The Dominion had just wiped their digital footprint, erasing everything they could use against them. Voss had walked away unscathed, confident in his power. And yet, Mercer knew something Voss didn't.

He had made a mistake.

Langley tapped furiously at his keyboard. "They scrubbed most of their network, but I found something—an old backup server, forgotten in the purge. It's not much, but it's something."

Mercer turned. "What's on it?"

Langley smirked. "A name."

Kane leaned in. "Whose?"

Langley hesitated before speaking. "Elliot Grayson. Former financial strategist. Disappeared six years ago."

Wilkes frowned. "And why does that matter?"

Langley turned his screen. "Because before he vanished, he was running The Dominion's offshore accounts. And if he's still alive, he knows where their money is."

Mercer's eyes narrowed. "Then we find him."

A Dangerous Lead

Grayson's last known location led them to a remote cabin in the mountains, far from the city's reach. It was the perfect place for someone who wanted to stay hidden.

"This feels wrong," Wilkes muttered as they parked a mile from the location. "If Grayson is so important, why leave a trail?"

Mercer checked his gun. "Because maybe he wants to be found."

They approached the cabin with caution. The air was eerily still, the crunch of their boots the only sound in the forest. Mercer raised a hand, signaling for a halt.

"Something's off," Kane muttered.

Langley frowned. "The cabin's power is still running. Someone's been here recently."

Mercer took the lead, pushing the door open. The inside was meticulously neat—too neat. As if someone had cleaned up before leaving. But then Mercer's gaze fell on the table in the center of the room.

A single laptop sat open, its screen displaying a paused video.

Wilkes pressed play.

The grainy footage showed a man—Elliot Grayson—bound to a chair, his face bruised and bloodied. A voice spoke from off-camera.

"You thought you could run, Elliot. But The Dominion never forgets."

A gunshot rang out. The screen went black.

Langley swallowed hard. "Well, that answers that."

Mercer's jaw clenched. "Not entirely. Someone wanted us to find this."

Kane picked up a note left beside the laptop. Four words were scrawled across the paper:

You're running out of time.

Wilkes exhaled. "This was a setup. Someone knew we were coming."

Langley's laptop beeped. "Mercer, we just tripped an alarm. We've got incoming."

Mercer's grip tightened on his gun. "Then we make our stand."

The Attack

Engines roared in the distance. Mercer and his team scrambled for cover as SUVs tore up the dirt road, headlights cutting through the darkness.

Gunfire erupted.

Mercer ducked behind an overturned table, returning fire. Kane and Wilkes moved in sync, taking down approaching hostiles with brutal efficiency.

"We're pinned!" Langley shouted, firing his pistol blindly.

Mercer's mind raced. This wasn't just an ambush. This was a message. The Dominion wasn't trying to kill them outright—they wanted them to suffer.

A familiar voice echoed through a nearby speaker.

"You should've stayed in the dark, Mercer. Now, you'll watch your team die one by one."

Mercer's blood ran cold.

Voss.

And then, from the trees, a new figure stepped into view. Dressed in a dark suit, his presence commanding, his smirk chilling.

"Mercer," Voss said smoothly. "Let's talk."

XXXIII

The Last Move

The headlights from the black SUVs cast long shadows against the trees, illuminating the cabin ruins like a stage set for execution. Mercer tightened his grip on his pistol, his breathing even despite the tension crackling in the air. Across from him, Director Henry Voss stood with a knowing smirk, his hands casually in his pockets, as if he weren't standing in the middle of an ambush.

"We both know how this ends, Mercer," Voss said smoothly. "You put up a fight, maybe take out a few of my men. But in the end? You fall. Just like the others."

Mercer's jaw clenched. "You sound just like Silas before he died choking on his own blood."

Voss chuckled, shaking his head. "Silas was predictable. He thought muscle alone could control The Dominion's interests. But we're not just an organization, Mercer. We're the foundation of this city. The judges, the politicians, the corporations—you think you can win against that?"

Langley's voice crackled in Mercer's earpiece. "I've got a backdoor into their comms. I can buy us two minutes, max. But we need to move—now."

Mercer didn't wait. In a flash, he fired, forcing Voss to dive behind an SUV. The gunfight erupted instantly. Kane and Wilkes moved like a well-oiled machine, taking down two of Voss' operatives as Mercer dove behind cover.

"Move to the right flank!" Kane barked, reloading. "We need to cut them off before reinforcements show up!"

Langley was already on it, hacking into the convoy's security system from his tablet. "I can disable their vehicles, but it'll take time!"

Bullets ricocheted off metal and shattered trees. The Dominion's men weren't just enforcers—they were trained killers, and they were closing in fast.

The Betrayal

Mercer took out a guard and pressed forward when a sharp pain seared through his side. A bullet had grazed him. He gritted his teeth, pushing through the pain. Then, from the corner of his eye, he saw something that stopped him cold.

Kane.

Standing still in the middle of the battlefield, staring right at Voss.

Mercer felt something shift in the air. A realization that settled like a gut punch.

Kane wasn't aiming at Voss. He was lowering his gun.

"Kane!" Mercer shouted, voice laced with disbelief.

Kane turned his head slowly. "Stand down, Mercer."

Time slowed. Mercer felt the betrayal settle deep in his bones, colder than any winter chill. "You were working with them? All this time?"

Kane exhaled. "It was never about winning, Mercer. It was about survival. You can't take down The Dominion. You either join them... or you die."

Wilkes turned his gun on Kane. "You son of a—"

Kane moved first. A single shot, straight into Wilkes' shoulder, sending him to the ground with a painful grunt. Mercer lunged at Kane, tackling him into the dirt. The two men rolled, fists flying, raw fury driving each strike.

"You sold us out!" Mercer growled, driving a punch into Kane's jaw.

Kane spit blood, his expression unreadable. "You're fighting a losing war, Mercer. I just chose the winning side."

The fight was brutal—two men who had once fought together now trying to tear each other apart. But then, in the distance, a new sound emerged.

Helicopter blades.

Langley's voice crackled in their earpieces. "Mercer, we've got incoming—air support! This isn't just an ambush. They're wiping us out!"

Voss, from his cover, laughed. "And that, gentlemen, is checkmate."

Mercer knew they were out of time. Wilkes was wounded, Langley was exposed, and The Dominion's full force was coming down on them.

Mercer made a decision. He grabbed Kane's own knife and drove it into his shoulder, forcing a pained scream from his former ally. "You chose wrong."

Then he grabbed Wilkes, hauling him to his feet. "Langley, now!"

Langley hit the detonator, triggering the explosives they had planted earlier. The SUVs went up in flames, sending The Dominion's operatives into chaos. Mercer, Wilkes, and Langley sprinted for the treeline, using the explosion as cover.

Kane, clutching his wounded shoulder, locked eyes with Mercer one last time. "You'll never stop them."

Mercer didn't look back. "Watch me."

As they disappeared into the forest, the fight wasn't over. It was just beginning.

XXXIV
Endgame Begins

The air was thick with tension as Mercer, Langley, and Wilkes trudged through the dense forest, using the cover of darkness to evade The Dominion's pursuit. Smoke from the earlier explosions still lingered in the air, mingling with the scent of pine and damp earth. Wilkes clutched his wounded shoulder, his breathing ragged.

"We need to find a safehouse," Langley muttered, keeping an eye on his GPS. "We're too exposed out here."

Mercer nodded. "We regroup, plan our next move. Voss thinks he's won, but we're not done yet."

Wilkes let out a dry chuckle. "And what's the next move? Taking down an untouchable man backed by an invisible empire? Sounds easy."

Langley's laptop beeped. He frowned. "We might not need to take Voss down directly. I just intercepted a transmission. Someone's trying to contact us."

Mercer narrowed his eyes. "Who?"

Langley hesitated. "It's coming from inside The Dominion. Someone on the inside wants to talk."

The Spy Within

They found an abandoned ranger station deep in the forest, setting up a makeshift command post. Langley worked furiously on his laptop, decrypting the incoming message.

Finally, a distorted voice crackled through the speakers. "Mercer. You're running out of time."

Mercer leaned forward. "Who are you?"

"Call me Wren," the voice replied. "I'm embedded inside The Dominion. Voss isn't the real power. He answers to someone else."

Wilkes gritted his teeth. "Oh, great. Another shadow pulling the strings."

Mercer remained focused. "Why are you helping us?"

A pause. "Because The Dominion is collapsing from the inside. There's a war coming, and you're in the middle of it. But if you want to end this, you need to go after the real leader."

Langley typed rapidly. "Who?"

A file appeared on screen. A name. A photograph.

Mercer's blood ran cold.

"Elliot Grayson is alive," Wren said. "And he's the true head of The Dominion."

A Ghost Returns

The room was deathly silent. Wilkes shook his head. "No way. We saw the video. He was executed."

"That was staged," Wren countered. "Grayson has been operating from the shadows, using Voss as a front. If you want to bring The Dominion down, you have to take him out."

Langley analyzed the data. "This is real. Bank records, encrypted messages, secret meetings—Grayson has been orchestrating everything from behind the curtain."

Mercer's grip tightened. "Where is he?"

Wren hesitated. "I can get you his location. But once you make a move, there's no turning back. He has his own security force, beyond The Dominion's usual men. If you fail, you won't get another chance."

Mercer exhaled, feeling the weight of what was coming. "Then we make sure we don't fail."

The Final Hunt

Grayson's safehouse was a private estate on the outskirts of Ridgewood—fortified, surrounded by security, and nearly impenetrable.

"We go in quiet," Mercer said, surveying the blueprints Langley had pulled up. "No alarms, no backup. Just us."

Wilkes grinned, checking his rifle. "Just the way I like it."

Langley exhaled. "This is it, isn't it? The final play."

Mercer met his gaze. "One way or another."

As they moved into position, Mercer felt something shift in the air. A storm was coming. One final battle to decide everything.

And this time, there would be no second chances.

XXXV

The Final Gambit

The cold wind howled through the trees as Mercer, Langley, and Wilkes crouched outside Grayson's fortified estate. The compound was a fortress—high walls, security cameras, motion sensors, and heavily armed guards patrolling the perimeter. It wasn't just a safehouse; it was a battlefield waiting to ignite.

Wilkes peered through the scope of his rifle. "Snipers on the roof. Looks like ex-military. This guy's not taking any chances."

Langley tapped furiously on his tablet. "I can disable some of their security, but only for a few minutes. If we're going in, we have to be fast."

Mercer's mind raced. They had one shot at this. "We split up. Wilkes, you take out the snipers. Langley, disrupt their comms and power. I'll breach from the north entrance."

Wilkes smirked. "You sure you want to go in alone?"

Mercer's expression was grim. "I'm not leaving without Grayson."

The Infiltration

The first sniper dropped silently, a suppressed round from Wilkes' rifle tearing through his skull. The second barely had time to register his partner's death before another bullet ended him.

Langley's fingers flew over his keyboard. "Power down in three... two... one."

The estate's exterior lights flickered, then went dark. Mercer moved swiftly through the shadows, reaching the northern gate. With practiced ease, he bypassed the lock and slipped inside.

The interior was eerily quiet. He pressed against the wall, gun raised, ears straining for movement. Footsteps. Two guards approaching. Mercer moved first—one quick shot to the knee of the first man, a brutal strike to the second's throat. Both crumpled before they could sound the alarm.

"I'm in," Mercer whispered into his comms. "Heading to the main floor."

Langley's voice crackled. "You need to hurry. Security's rebooting faster than expected."

Mercer rounded a corner—

And walked straight into an ambush.

The Trap

A dozen laser sights painted his chest in red dots. The guards had been waiting.

From the staircase, a slow, deliberate set of footsteps echoed. And then, emerging from the shadows, came the man himself—Elliot Grayson.

He looked older than the last known photos, but his sharp eyes gleamed with intelligence and something darker. "Detective Mercer," Grayson said smoothly. "I expected you sooner."

Mercer clenched his jaw. "You're a hard man to find."

Grayson smirked. "That was the idea. But here you are, standing in my house. And now you have a choice."

The guards tightened their grip on their weapons. Mercer's pulse pounded, but he kept his expression neutral. "What kind of choice?"

Grayson descended the stairs, stopping a few feet away. "You've been chasing ghosts, Mercer. You think bringing me down ends The Dominion? You don't understand. We don't die. We adapt. We evolve. Even if you kill me, there will always be another."

Mercer's grip on his gun tightened. "Then I'll keep killing."

Grayson chuckled. "Or, you could join us."

Silence.

Mercer blinked. "You think I'd work for you?"

"You already do," Grayson said. "Every time you follow the trail, every time you play this game, you're doing exactly what we want. Controlled chaos. A distraction while the real work continues elsewhere. But you're smart, Mercer. Smarter than most. That's why I'm offering you a seat at the table."

Mercer's stomach turned. "Not a chance."

Grayson sighed. "Pity. Then I'm afraid this is where your story ends."

He snapped his fingers.

Gunfire erupted.

The Last Stand

Mercer dove for cover as bullets shredded the air around him. Wilkes' voice crackled through the comms. "We're coming in hot! Hang tight!"

Mercer rolled behind a marble pillar, returning fire. Two guards went down. Then an explosion rocked the estate—Wilkes had breached the southern wall.

"Move, move!" Langley shouted.

Guards scrambled, but the tide was shifting. Mercer seized the moment, pushing forward. He spotted Grayson retreating up the stairs.

"Grayson's on the move!" Mercer yelled.

Wilkes tossed him a fresh clip. "Then let's end this."

As Mercer sprinted after Grayson, he knew one thing for certain:

One way or another, this was the final battle.

XXXVI

The Last Stand

The grand staircase loomed ahead, bathed in the glow of fire from the burning wreckage behind Mercer. Elliot Grayson had retreated to his private quarters at the top, his last stronghold. Mercer sprinted forward, his breath ragged, his gun heavy in his grip.

Wilkes' voice crackled over the comms. "We've cleared the lower levels. Reinforcements are coming in hot—this has to end now, Mercer!"

Mercer reached the top of the stairs and kicked open the heavy double doors. Inside, Grayson stood behind a mahogany desk, pouring himself a drink.

"You made it," Grayson said smoothly. "I was starting to think you wouldn't."

Mercer raised his gun. "Game's over, Grayson."

Grayson smirked, unbothered. "Is it? Because from where I stand, the game hasn't even begun."

A Battle of Wits

Mercer took a step forward. "Your empire is burning. Your men are dead or running. You lost."

Grayson took a sip of his drink. "You think taking me down ends The Dominion? Mercer, we're not a man. We're not a building. We're an idea. And you can't kill an idea."

Mercer gritted his teeth. "Watch me."

He pulled the trigger.

A deafening bang echoed through the room—but Grayson was faster. He dove behind his desk, a bullet shattering the glass of a liquor cabinet behind him. A hidden panel on the wall slid open, revealing a mounted shotgun. Grayson grabbed it and fired, forcing Mercer to dive for cover.

"Do you know why you've always been one step behind, Mercer?" Grayson called out. "Because you fight for the past. The Dominion fights for the future."

Mercer reloaded. "That future looks pretty bleak right now."

The Betrayal

Footsteps pounded outside the door. Wilkes burst in, gun raised. "We've got to move! The whole estate is rigged to blow!"

Grayson, bleeding from a graze on his shoulder, let out a laugh. "You didn't think I'd let you take me alive, did you?"

Mercer fired again, this time hitting Grayson in the leg. He collapsed, groaning in pain.

Langley's voice came through the comms. "Mercer, the servers—he's uploading everything. The Dominion's plans, their assets, all of it. If we can stop the upload—"

Mercer grabbed Grayson by the collar. "Shut it down!"

Grayson coughed, smirking through the pain. "Even if you kill me, Mercer, it's too late. Someone else will take my place. The Dominion doesn't fall."

Mercer slammed him against the desk. "Then I'll make sure you don't live to see it."

Before Mercer could pull the trigger, a shot rang out—

Wilkes stumbled back, a bullet ripping through his chest.

Mercer's blood ran cold as he turned—

Kane.

The man Mercer had once called his ally stood in the doorway, gun smoking. His expression was unreadable.

"Step away from Grayson," Kane said.

Mercer clenched his jaw. "You traitorous son of a—"

"No time for speeches, Mercer." Kane kept his gun raised. "Grayson is more valuable alive than dead."

Wilkes groaned from the floor, blood pooling beneath him. Mercer's grip on his gun tightened.

"You were one of us," Mercer growled.

Kane shook his head. "I survived. That's what matters. And if you want to live, you'll let him go."

The estate trembled—the explosives were about to detonate.

Langley's voice cracked over the comms. "Mercer, you have thirty seconds!"

Mercer had a choice to make.

Kane smirked. "Choose wisely."

Epilogue – The Cost Of Shadows

The flames devoured Grayson's estate, consuming the last remnants of his empire. The explosion had sent a shockwave through the forest, scattering debris and smoke into the night sky. Mercer stood at the edge of the wreckage, his face smeared with soot and blood, his body aching from the battle.

Wilkes was slumped against a fallen beam, his hand pressing against his wounded chest. "Hell of a way to go out," he muttered, spitting blood onto the dirt. "Think we got 'em all?"

Mercer glanced at the destruction. "Grayson's gone. But The Dominion? That's another question."

Langley approached, his tablet in hand, his face pale. "I managed to intercept one last transmission before the servers went down. The Dominion's leadership is fractured, but they're not dead. They'll rebuild. They always do."

Mercer exhaled, wiping his brow. "Then we stay ready. Because this isn't over."

A rustling in the trees made them snap to attention. Guns raised. But instead of another enemy, it was Kane—stumbling, bloodied, his hands raised in surrender.

"Mercer..." Kane coughed. "It's done. I... I was never with them. I had to play both sides to survive."

Wilkes scoffed. "And we're just supposed to believe that? After you shot me?"

Kane met Mercer's eyes. "I made a choice back there. I didn't kill you. That has to count for something."

Mercer studied him for a long moment before lowering his gun. "Get out of here, Kane. If I ever see you again... it won't end like this."

Kane nodded, vanishing into the shadows like a ghost.

Langley let out a breath. "What now?"

Mercer looked out at the burning ruins. "Now? We disappear. Lay low. Because if The Dominion isn't dead, they'll come looking for us. And next time... we'll be ready."

The team walked away from the wreckage, fading into the fog. The war wasn't over.

But the first battle had been won.